The Orchard

ALSO BY BENJAMIN TAMMUZ

Minotaur (New American Library, 1981)

Requiem for Na'Aman (New American Library, 1982)

THE ORCHARD

a novella by

Benjamin Tammuz

Translated by Richard Flantz

Copper Beech Press

The publication of this book was made possible by grants from the Rhode Island State Council on the Arts and the National Endowment for the Arts, a Federal agency, in Washington, D.C.

This translation was made possible by the help of the Institute for the Translation of Hebrew Literature.

Cover illustration courtesy of the Annmary Brown Memorial, Brown University.

For information, address the publisher:
Copper Beech Press
Box 1852
Brown University
Providence, Rhode Island 02912

Library of Congress Cataloging in Publication Data
Tammuz, Benjamin, 1919 -
The orchard.

Translation of: ha-Pardes.
I. Title.
PJ5054.T317P313 1984 892.4'3 84-15571
ISBN 0-914278-43-6 (pbk.)

First Edition
Printed in the United States of America

The Very Reverend Father
Basil Theodore [illegible]

A man kindles a light for himself at night,
When he has died yet is still alive.
The sleeper takes light from the dead;
He that is awake takes light from the sleeper.

— Heraclitus

Dean of the Greek Orthodox Church
in New England and New York
the year of the Lord
One Thousand Nine Hundred
and Ninety

1 Obadiah's Beginnings

Several generations ago there lived in the land of Russia a Jew who had two sons. The elder was named Obadiah, and the younger, Daniel. I know and can recount everything about Obadiah — everything, that is, one person can recount about another — from the day of his arrival in the land of Israel. But of what happened before his arrival I know only by hearsay.

And this is what I have heard: Obadiah's father was the son of a well-to-do family, but in his youth he pursued wild follies, though his pockets were filled with gold and he was blessed with all of the seven wisdoms. When he turned twenty, he got on a train traveling east and arrived in Constantinople, where he stayed for some five years or more. He bought himself a house on a high hill, its windows looking out upon the tongue of sea where Russian ships made their way to the south. He, too, participated in the commerce of these ships and even made a fortune, for in those days Constantinople was a city that ruled the seas, a mistress of kingdoms, but there's no point in expanding on this — all of us know it.

After some time he brought a woman, a daughter of common people in Antioch, into his house to be his housekeeper. She was young and plump, her skin as fair as that of Russian girls, but even more so. And since he was young, and the woman delighted his palate with spicy foods, as is the custom of Turks raised on the spices of the East, their food being fatty and fried, wrapped in vine leaves and emitting the fragrance of muscat nuts, saffron, cumin, honey, and frankincense, the master of the house was regaled in delights and lacked nothing save a wife. The woman came and lay with him, as is the custom of the lowly, who if they serve in a man's kitchen have no inhibitions about also serving in his bed.

Such was the conception and birth of Obadiah. He was born of the union of a maidservant and a wealthy young man, without the ceremony and sanctity of marriage, in a wealthy home where nothing was lacking save the moral virtues. And when Obadiah was five or six years old his father began getting bored among the Turks. Due to his easy successes in business his desire for money abated; and since his housekeeper was not the most intelligent of women, he grew tired of her and decided to return to his homeland. Before leaving for Russia he had the house registered in the housekeeper's name and settled a sum of money upon her and rid himself of her honorably and without tears. But he took his son Obadiah with him, for the heart of a Jew cleaves to his offspring, even though they be sons of a shameless Gentile woman.

Many years later I heard from Mehmet Effendi, my Turkish friend and the owner of the orchard where Obadiah worked as overseer and watchman, that Obadiah had told him of his parting from his mother. On that last day in Constantinople his father hired a carriage loaded with two or three crates of gold and silverware and clothes, took Obadiah in his arms, and set off with him towards the port. The woman, Obadiah's mother, peeped out at them from the doorway. When the carriage had gone a short distance from the house, the woman started walking in the wake of the horses, weeping. And there was not one man in all that great city, not one man or one woman out of all the myriads of inhabitants milling around in the streets, to take his mother's side or to ask her what distressed her and why she was crying. All that time his father was holding him close and trying to distract him with affectionate words, but Obadiah's eyes were fixed on his weeping mother, who walked behind the carriage at a distance, until they reached the port and climbed the gangway into the ship. From that day on he never saw her again.

When Obadiah's father returned to Russia, he learned that his parents had passed away and left him an estate with houses and money. He gathered all his great wealth together and several months later brought home an eligible woman, the daughter of exceedingly wealthy rabbis, an erudite Jewish woman who spoke fluent French and played the piano, did embroidery on silk and painted small pictures on porcelain tiles, as was the custom in those days. On the day of his father's wedding the boy was taken from the house by one of the servants to a distant country estate, and there he remained for about a month. After that he was returned to his father's house, and from that time on they were not parted until the day

Obadiah left for the land of Israel, at the age of about twenty.

They were good years, those years Obadiah spent with his father in the land of Russia. The woman his father had married was good-hearted, and she raised Obadiah together with her own son, who was born at the end of their first year of marriage. She instructed her own son to call Obadiah "brother," even though she had been told that the boy who had been brought from Turkey was an adopted orphan. And so it happened that Obadiah's brother, Daniel, was never misled and saw Obadiah as his own brother, as was really the case.

But Obadiah secretly hated his brother and his father and also turned against his father's wife, who bore his caprices patiently and pitied him as one pities an orphan who is bitter at heart.

When Daniel, Obadiah's brother, turned six and a tutor was brought to the house to teach him to read and write, Obadiah was still having difficulties with reading, refusing to sit down to lessons with his tutor and rebuffing the goodness encircling him. But when little Daniel started excelling in his studies and reciting the Songs of Zion by heart, Obadiah grew jealous and in his fury suddenly started driving his tutor, until within several months he completed what he had not covered in several years. But after that he stopped studying again and took no more interest in learning; he gave his time to hunting and fishing, and loved the dogs and the horses of the estate, in whose company he spent all his days.

One evening Obadiah did not come to dinner, and at night he was not to be found in his bed. The servants went looking for him and found him asleep in the stable. When his father asked him for an explanation, he refused to give one. And when this happened a second time, his father ordered the servants not to wake him but to leave him there sleeping.

And once, Turkish merchants visited their city and stayed at at the hostelry for a week, and when they left, Obadiah vanished and was not seen for several days. And when the family had already given him up for lost, one of the Turks took Obadiah to the house and told them how the boy had stuck to them like a shadow, refusing to be parted from them even though the Turks had urged him to return home. But the merchants had begun to fear that the police would find a pretext to say they had kidnapped a Russian boy so as to make him a slave in their own country, and so this Turk had returned him to his father's house against his will.

The members of the household saw that the boy longed to be independent and wanted a place to hide in, so they built him living quarters above the stable, all his own. Even his food was taken to him there, and no one visited him, so that he wouldn't be disturbed or want to run away again. Only Daniel, his little brother, didn't like this separation and would climb up to Obadiah's room, seeking his company. But after being turned away two or three times, he wiped his tears and didn't climb the ladder again.

Several years passed, until it was time for Daniel's bar mitzvah, and the whole house filled with the bustle of festivities. Women busily cooked dishes and servants hung lamps on the veranda. On the morning of that day everyone went to the synagogue. At noon they came back to sit down at the table, and one of the servants was sent to the attic to get Obadiah but didn't find him there. They sent some of the delicacies from the dinner up to his room — sweetmeat and wine and candy — and placed them on his table, so he could eat them when he came back.

The next day, when they took Obadiah breakfast, they found his bed still made. It obviously hadn't been slept in. They told his father. The father went to look in his desk drawer, and found his purse missing.

They never saw or heard from Obadiah again, nor did they receive any sign or rumor of him.

At the time Obadiah was about twenty years old.

The period during which Obadiah vanished from his family's ken was also the period during which Obadiah became known to me. And from the day I first saw him until the day he died, not one week passed, and sometimes not even one day, without my seeing him. From here on my story is based on firsthand knowledge, and I shall no longer need to make use of rumors absorbed from the air.

2 A Citrus Orchard with Some Pomegranates and Figs

One morning, more than forty years ago, old Mehmet Effendi, an affluent and propertied Turk who was highly respected among us, came to see me with strange news. For many years he had had a kind of serf or slave, an Arab, who oversaw his orchard and lived in it, next to the packing shed; one day the man had been found dead in the orchard, and now my acquaintance had hired a new man to replace him. But this new man did not understand this country's language — he spoke Turkish and also knew the language of the country I came from, Russia; the man was educated and intelligent and capable of learning the secrets of the soil, until he could attain almost to my degree of achievement. So the old man told me that day and asked me to come to his orchard with him to speak with his new employee and to instruct him, for which I would receive whatever remuneration I asked.

You're joking with me, Mehmet Effendi, I said to him. If your man speaks Russian, it means he's a Jew. Why should you hire a Jew if you want to teach someone the secrets of the orchard? The wages of Jews are high. You kept your previous worker, the one who died, for a bowl of lentils and a couple of pennies. Explain this to me, Mehmet Effendi.

He's not a Jew but an Ishmaelite from Turkey, said the old man. And the dead man who served me for thirty years was like a brother to me. He ate my food and wore my clothes. I even bought him a wife with my own money, and it isn't my fault that she was sickly and died on him a long time ago. Now come with me — don't say no.

I got into his carriage and about an hour after leaving my orchard we arrived at his, and together we mounted the stone steps to the top floor, which looked out over a pool of water. We went into the parlor. There I saw Obadiah for the first time. He was seated on cushions on the stone settee next to the wall, a cup of coffee in his hand. The old man's wife and Luna, their daughter, were peeping out at us from the kitchen doorway, awaiting a word from the master of the house. Mehmet Effendi immediately called for coffee and sweetmeats and bowls full of pomegranate grains, and I soon started wondering about what I was seeing, discovering a little and losing twice as much. Obadiah was presented to me by the name "Abdullah." I was told he was a Turk who had spent several years in Russia and now wanted to live in Palestine and practice the trade of orchardry. The old man praised me to the skies and enjoined Abdullah to listen to my every word, since there was no one so versed in trees and their diseases as I, or anyone who knew so well the secrets of irrigation and grafting and the other work in the orchard. And when he had ceased his praises, I asked Abdullah if he had ever had anything to do with agriculture.

He answered that he knew horses and animals and that he had grown up on a farming estate, and though he had never worked in agriculture, he was willing to learn and had strong hopes that he would not disappoint his employer.

His speech was dry, almost short, and I did not cease wondering at this amazing scene, in which the employee spoke in his master's presence as if he were claiming a debt or was to inherit from him in the future. For Mehmet Effendi was a firm man, one who knew how to deal with people and who was accustomed to their doing his will.

For a moment it occurred to me that the old man had settled on Abdullah as a bridegroom for his daughter, for the pair had no sons. The son born to them years ago had died in his youth; and the girl, Luna, was not from his wife's womb, but an adopted child and their only heir. But I immediately banished this idle fancy. Had the old man wished to marry Luna to Abdullah, would he have hired him as overseer and watchman in his orchard? True, by his clothes and manners one could see that Abdullah was not of the lower classes, but since such a healthy and handsome youth was willing to lower himself to a job that was not one of the finest, his pockets must be empty. And why should the Turk give the heiress of his great wealth to a penniless man? Who of the young men of the region, of the sons of the wealthy and the notables, would not have rejoiced to take Luna for a wife? Not only because of the wealth that awaited her after the death of her foster parents, but also because of her great beauty, the like of which one does not see today; nor do I recall that even in those days I had ever seen so excellent a girl as she. The one flaw she did have, that of dumbness, he would not have discovered for himself without addressing her. Luna never opened her mouth to say a word.

So what was happening here? I asked myself. Time would remove the screens of the secret, I believed, and I accepted my friend's proposal. Abdullah was not the first man, or the last, to learn from me the secrets of raising citrus fruits. And since in those days I was undergoing financial difficulties — my orchard was young and did not yield fruit yet, while demanding water and manure — I earned a living by overseeing the orchards of others and by teaching the trade to laymen. In those days I was almost the only man in our parts who had studied agronomy abroad before arriving in the country.

And since I'd agreed, we went down to the orchard to walk around it and inspect its condition. It was an orchard of inestimable size, full of citrus trees, some of them oranges, some lemons, and there were even a few citrons there. And among them, and at the fringes, several groups of fig and pomegranate trees; and above the veranda over the pool wound an ancient vine of Dabuki grapes, and in the summer season, when its clusters hung overhead, bees would come there by the hundreds, and those seated on the porch would hold straw swatters in their hands to chase the bees away.

When we entered the orchard, it was as if night had engulfed us in darkness. It was so dense that I will not be exaggerating if I say the trees were no more than two meters apart and one could not walk among them without getting scratched or breaking a path as if through swampy undergrowth. Except the vegetation in the orchard, and especially the undergrowth, was dry, tangled, and thorny; and only a small green treetop crowned each tree to enjoy the sunlight.

In my orchard the trees were planted four meters apart, and had I been fortunate enough to see it yield fruit, I could possibly have attained to a hundred kilos a tree. Mehmet Effendi's trees yielded possibly no more than twenty kilos a tree, and since I was speaking in Russian to Obadiah, whom I still called "Abdullah" at the time, I was not afraid that the old man might understand me, and stated my view explicitly to my new pupil. There's no cure for this orchard, I said, other than rooting it up. And until its owner agrees to root it up, there's still a lot of vacant land in his possession, all around it, to plant new orchards in, with proper spaces between the trees. On that occasion I explained to him the reason for the drying up and the difficulties of cultivation. If you irrigate an orchard such as this abundantly, I told him, you bring decay, and if you scrimp on the irrigation, you bring dryness and death. There was no cure for the Turk's estate.

Mehmet Effendi pretended to be deaf, but I'm sure he understood what I said. He walked along beside us in silence and occasionally smiled under his mustache. He was a cunning Turk, but good-hearted and even-tempered.

From the questions Obadiah asked, I could see I was dealing with an intelligent man, one who knew what to ask and whose speech was measured; except there was something dark and threatening in his speech. When he asked a question, he was like an interrogator; and when he replied, it was as though he had said: I've understood, don't talk too much.

From that difficult progress of ours through the darkness of the orchard that first day with Obadiah, I remember something that happened two or three times, and on that occasion I was not sure if I had really seen what I had seen, or if the darkness had confused me. Afterwards I got used to it, and I knew it had not been a delusion: when we reached a place between a row of parallel trees, whose branches did not hide what was before us, we suddenly glimpsed in the distance the figure of Luna. The first time, I saw her standing with her back to us, as if lost in thought. She immediately vanished. And another time, several minutes later, I saw her leaning with one hand on a tree trunk, looking at us. Then, too, she suddenly vanished, as suddenly as she had appeared. I do not know if Mehmet Effendi and Obadiah also noticed her. In any case, there was no sign that they had seen her. And since it was not my business to stick my nose into something that was no affair of mine, I did not wonder at this young girl wandering around among the trees, appearing in this place and that at one and the same time. Perhaps there are two Lunas, I said to myself.

Here I ought to remark on one thing before returning to the course of events: in those days the daughters of the Muslims used to dress with extreme modesty, and the cloth covering their bodies would suffice today to sew dresses for five modern girls. Needless to say, a girl like Luna, the daughter of a Turkish man of property, was covered from head to toe, with several layers wrapped around her shoulders and her waist and no skin showing, save a gleaming white hand's-breadth of forehead and cheeks and eyes blazing in the middle. Nevertheless I am ready to swear that, in the flashing glimpse I had of her in the orchard then, she looked entirely naked. That is to say, there is no doubt that she was dressed most decently, except this was how she looked to the observer. Or did it seem like that only to me, because I was very young then? At any rate, there was nudity about her always. Even when she moved through her father's parlor, serving refreshments to guests.

Be that as it may, clouds were gathering in the clear winter sky. And before we fled from the rain, I managed to show Obadiah several diseased fruits and to warn him to be sure that, whenever he saw an orange covered with a rusty hue or a lemon turned silvery or a grapefruit that had changed color until it was a kind of ripe-olive shade, he was to dust immediately with strong sulphur.

And then it started raining, and we returned to the house.

3 1915, the Year of the Locusts

About a year after Obadiah's arrival the world war broke out. It happened in summer, in 1914, and the orchard-owners got into a thorough panic. In England people didn't have the time to enjoy oranges, and, furthermore, the English government had mobilized all its merchant ships for the war. And England was our biggest market. Not only England but Hamburg, too, stopped buying fruit. And Russia, too, which had begun buying oranges in fair quantities, its trade with us already reaching a tenth of all the fruit we sent out of the Ottoman Empire, was also swept into the war, and the growers were very worried.

To tell the truth, I admit that I didn't care. My orchard would yield fruit only in another year and a half; and by then, we said to ourselves, the war would be over and forgotten, leaving behind only the memory of a bad dream. At the same time, the growers didn't want to neglect their plantations, and I had my hands full, working both for myself and for others. And since, as I have said, most of my income then came from giving instruction and overseeing the orchards of others, my situation, rather than deteriorating, improved. I would be able to hold out even more than a year and a half. For I was a bachelor and already had a reputation as an expert.

As for Mehmet Effendi's orchard, I got little satisfaction from it; not from the orchard or from its overseer, Obadiah. He was a strange fellow, Obadiah. At first glance he seemed to understand whatever I explained to him, but only in theory. In practice he didn't lift a finger.

It's not an orchard you've got here, I used to say to him, it's a ruin. A hundred trees to the *dunam* is like a death sentence for an orchard. No yield and no future.

And he listened, understood, saw my orchard — fifty trees to the *dunam* — growing and flourishing, a delight to the eyes, and did not even bother to propose either an uprooting or a new planting to his master. Like a blind horse tied to a water wheel, he tramped through the vast orchard, watering when watering was necessary, hoeing when hoeing was necessary — all according to the year's schedule and according to necessity, it seemed — not aware that he was driving nails into a coffin. True, it wasn't his orchard. But when does an intelligent man saw off the branch he sits on? It was certain that in another year or two, at the very most five years, there would be no work here, so was it worth it? While it was possible, with exactly the same amount of effort, to come out with twice or four times the profit!

But just as I got no satisfaction from my pupil, I was very pleased with my own orchard. Each morning I could see how the trunks of the trees were thickening, how gleaming bright was the green of the leaves, their rustling bearing good tidings: there would be fruit, too, and wages for my labor.

In the village of Sumeil, a two-hours' walk from my orchard, there was a widow, Sarah-Itah Falman by name, with a lot of little children. Her husband had died in his orchard, of sunstroke. Were it not for that widow's bravery and the beauty of that orchard, I would not be afraid to say that in all the land of Israel there was not a Jew more worthy of praise than I, in terms of both agricultural knowledge and the stubborn stand of a farmer faithfully working his land.

Such was the state of affairs during the first year of that war. They were good days, beyond the shadow of a doubt: I was young, an expert with a reputation; the country around was clean and quiet within a vast calm that gave off the scent of blossoming and of water flowing in channels; pleasant sounds rose into the air — the sounds of pulsing wells and of animals wandering through uncultivated land. Far, far away, in the lands of the Gentiles, Ham was striking Japheth, as has been their custom for generations upon generations; but to these orchards the sounds of war did not come, and the roots of the trees sucked and were sated; the foliage turned green in the sun and the fruit swelled at the base of the flower and a wonderful fragrance hovered over the face of the earth. Cursed be the day of my birth and cursed be the hour of my decision to link my life with citrus trees!

On the eleventh day of March in 1915, an east wind blew in the morning and when I went out to my trees, I was not overly surprised by the khamsin and thought sadly that I would have to move up the date of the next watering, because the soil under my feet had immediately shown signs of dryness and cracking. I bent down to the ground and crumbled a bit of earth between my thumb and forefinger, as if trying to make sure there really was a khamsin in the air. And as I was bending down over the earth, a rustle reached my ears. I had never heard a sound like that, but I did not need to straighten up in order to know what was happening. Some primeval voice — some knowledge I had known before my birth, as it were — told me clearly what was happening around me. Or perhaps it was an old memory, a memory of something I had read in the book of the prophet Joel, when I was yet a boy in my father's house: "A day of darkness and gloom, a day of clouds and thick darkness, as the morning spread upon the mountains, a great people and a strong . . . a fire devoureth before them and behind them a flame burneth; the land is as the garden of Eden before them, and behind them a desolate wilderness. . . . The vine is dried up, and the fig tree languisheth; the pomegranate tree, the palm tree also, and the apple tree, even all the trees of the field, are withered. . . ."

Swarms of locusts driven by the wind fell at my feet and spread out among the trees, and I remember, as if it were today, my first feelings on seeing those detested insects: neither alarm nor fear overcame me that first moment, but a sense of terrible insult; by what right — I wanted to scream madly — by what right do you come to my orchard, to my plot of land? Who gave you permission? Get out of here, you abominations of nature!

Of course, I did not shout. Overcome with amazement, mute and helpless, I gazed at the swarming cloud, and at the same time my brain started weaving strategies of battle and destruction. I knew — for I had learned it from the many books I had studied — that I still had several weeks' grace. Not many —perhaps two or three. Cool and quiet on the outside, although my heart was full of foreboding, I started making preparations right away. Fuming with anger, I left the orchard to the insects and rode off on my donkey to Jaffa to buy sheets of tin. The locusts that had arrived in my orchard were not hungry. The real danger would develop from the larvae, which would emerge from the eggs after this generation mated with its females and died. And until then I had some two or three weeks.

Day in and day out, I traveled to Jaffa to locate and bring

back sheets of tin, and in the afternoon hours I diligently killed, with a stick, the locusts mating in my orchard. While they were mating, they did not flee from me, and with one blow I would smash them, two by two. The females that escaped my stick would fly, already fertilized, to the fallow beyond the orchard, there to lay their eggs.

I instructed Mehmet Effendi as to what he should do in his orchard, and I told Obadiah to hire every man he could get, to do as he did — strike, kill, and destroy. And, in fact, quite a considerable number of people gathered in the old man's orchard, and even Mehmet Effendi himself and his old wife went out into the orchard with sticks in their hands. That much of a fright I had been able to put into them. Only Luna did not step outside the house and would sometimes look out from the window of the parlor, gazing at the tribe of excited people in the orchard. Toward noon she would come out to bathe in the pool, in a special dress. My blood boiled within me, and I spoke my mind to Obadiah and told him that the girl was acting like a madwoman. But Obadiah smiled. It was rare to see a smile on his lips. Perhaps once every half-year. And here, now, he had found a moment to smile.

When I advised Mehmet Effendi to procure sheets of tin to put around his orchard and in this way to protect the trees from the larvae when they emerged from their eggs, the old Turk laughed. Where can one find enough sheets of tin in this country to surround my orchard? he said. And he was certainly right. I was sure, then, that his orchard was lost, whereas my orchard, which was small, would be protected by the tin I had managed to collect during these two weeks. Thanks to my great diligence I had managed to surround my plot completely with a fence almost a meter in height, made of sheets of tin stuck into the earth and firmly attached to each other.

Then came the hour of emergence. Several hours after emerging from the eggs, the newly born locusts turned into larvae, which looked like a cross between a large ant and a small worm. They traveled in large battalions, and their appetite grew from hour to hour. At first they ate grass and soft leaves. When they finished these, they turned to the branches and the bark of the trees. Finally, they swallowed each other: the large ones devoured the small. If a fire was lit in the path of the traveling larvae, they managed to slip through between the centers of the blaze, and if there was no way to pass by, leaders appeared among them to guide the battalions and warn them of danger. And if we had thought that streams, channels, or rivers would stop them, there was the incident at the Yarkon River to prove us wrong: they made a bridge, over which millions of them passed to and fro from one bank to the other.

With my stick in my hand, striking out like a madman in a dance of lunatics, I ran about my orchard, which was protected by smooth sheets of tin, to see what I could still do that I hadn't done yet. The larvae tried to climb up the sheets but slid backwards and fell to the earth. Then they came back and tried in another place, and fell again. But not all the sheets of tin I had bought were smooth. Some were rusty and had protuberances on them, and also some of the joins I had made between sheets didn't hold up. The battalions of larvae pressed on them in force, climbed and burst in between the sheets, and here and there broke into the orchard.

Each day a new generation of larvae emerged, and each day the food available to them decreased and their appetite grew. Finally they ate the leaves of the cacti and the bitter branches of the eucalypts.

It was only at that stage of the campaign that I realized my error. In the orchards that had not been fenced in with tin, the larvae got in easily, ate only the leaves, and continued on their way; such an orchard was only slightly injured. But in places where a fence had stood in their way for a long time, their hunger had grown. And when they did burst in, they finished everything: leaves, branches, and bark, until they had wrought total destruction.

Thus was Mehmet Effendi's orchard saved, and thus, in a few short hours, doom fell upon my life's work. And when I was struck down with madness, I would rave and say that Mehmet Effendi's orchard had been saved because the larvae got sick of his rotten trees and his dry and withered grass, while my orchard had been an innocent sacrificial victim, because its fresh greenness was a delight to the palate, a delicacy of angels on the tables of the Devil's offspring.

In my madness I blamed Luna and claimed the stillness that rose from her like a vapor had aroused the wrath of the angels of destruction, and her nakedness had angered the demons, and it was she who had put an end to my happiness.

For many months I was shrouded in darkness; and when I was well again, I returned to the land of the living. But I never returned to my prior status or strength. From that year on I was a different man.

4 I Decline to Obadiah's Degree, and We Become Friends

A tree struck by lightning may be completely consumed by fire, leaving nothing but a charred trunk, a kind of monument that stands and is eroded by wind and rain. But sometimes nature plays tricks with it, and after a while a green shoot will spring out of the burned trunk. The tree will never yield fruit, but it will exhibit this strange greenness — unnaturally, as it were. From this green shoot will bud — not in their season — various kinds of blossoms that are a wonder to behold. And he who understands will feel grief at the sight of such an unnatural flowering. But he who does not understand may possibly believe the tree is renewing its life.

My acquaintances believed that I had fully recuperated. Mehmet Effendi, God reward him, spoiled me as if I were his son. He fought off my creditors and moved heaven and earth in the Seraia, the government building in Jaffa, until he had managed to absolve me of most of my debts; but under the circumstances I got out by the skin of my teeth, naked and destitute, at the mercy of the heavens.

When I returned to the land of the living, I found myself dwelling in the packing shed in Mehmet Effendi's orchard, with Obadiah for a neighbor. In the first days I was like the cock in the fable, eating and doing nothing else at all, but soon I dragged myself off the mat I had been lying on and went out into the orchard — a horrible sight: the orchard and, apparently, I myself.

I remember I tried to think, to come up with a solution to a problem that wasn't clear to me. It seems I wanted to save the disaster-stricken people around me, but to my amazement I saw no disaster-stricken people — only people carrying on as if nothing had happened. Obadiah did his work as if not a thing had occurred; Mehmet Effendi and his wife received their guests and Luna kept looking out the window, bathing in the pool and wandering through the orchard, appearing for some moments and then vanishing again for the rest of the day.

And instead of pulling myself together like a man and warning them of the situation they were in, I was overcome by feeble-mindedness — the same weakness that destroyed the passion for action in me for the rest of my life, and from which I was never cured — and I went to Obadiah and asked him to tell me what to do. And from then on Obadiah would tell me what work to do each day, and I would carry it out, like an apprentice at his master's bidding. And from the day when Obadiah became my master, the barriers collapsed in the packing shed — from then on we took our afternoon nap together, under the thatch, and together we smoked from the nargileh in the morning. If Mehmet Effendi wasn't entertaining guests, we sat with him on the porch of his house, above the pool; and if he was occupied, we smoked our cigarettes in the packing shed, chatting and joking until we fell asleep.

Naturally, I couldn't help seeing and knowing what was going on between Obadiah and Luna; for my neighbor would rise from his mat on numerous occasions, in the middle of the night or in the early hours of the morning, and sneak out like a cat and walk into the orchard, where he stayed for an hour or two. And when he returned, he didn't speak to me, even when I was awake, and would curl up under his blanket and fall asleep.

Once I asked him how he spoke with Luna, for she was dumb. Obadiah smiled and gave me a sly glance and said: Oh, my master and teacher, was it not you who taught me to understand the language of the earth — if it is dry, it must be watered, and if it is moist, it is not yet ready to drink water? Was it not you who told me that the trees do not speak, that one must observe them to see if it is time to prune the dry branches? Why then do you ask about Luna? She is like the earth and the trees. Only look at her, and you know what she wants.

There must be two Lunas, I once again said to myself. One whom I know and one who is hidden from me, the one of whom Obadiah speaks.

Another time he told me the secret of her origin. She was the daughter of eminent notables, of the very first families who had lived in this country generations ago. Her parents had been killed by bandits, and only Luna had survived, and Mehmet Effendi had taken her into his home when she was still a child.

Some time after the days I am telling about now, I heard from Mehmet Effendi, a short while before he died, that Luna's parents had been his neighbors for many years and that Luna had been neither deaf nor dumb in her parents' home, becoming as she was now only after their deaths.

During that period I heard many stories, from which I also learned a little of what I have told about Obadiah's beginnings, before his coming to this land. But in all his stories he avoided mention of his father and spoke with love only of his mother, and of his being a true Muslim Ishmaelite, Abdullah by name.

We spent many days telling stories, until the war — which till then had been something distant — came closer to us with its turmoil. We did not suffer from the hunger rife in the country, for in the orchard we raised vegetables and chickens and so we lacked nothing. But by decree of the Turks the ancient cypresses around the orchard were cut down, and their trunks were taken off to sawmills, to the furnaces of trains and to the cooking ovens of the retreating army. Since I was a Jew, Mehmet Effendi was forced to hide me because of the expulsion decree against Jews, and during the last days of the war I almost did not stick my nose outside the bounds of the orchard. Afterwards we heard the sound of cannons to the north, and people coming from the other side of the Yarkon told us that the English had crossed the river near Bedas's orchard.

5 Mehmet Effendi's Orchard Is Put Up for Sale

After the defeat of the Turks, when the English came in and occupied the country, I knew I was free to come and go as I wished, but I did not want to move from where I was. When Obadiah didn't tell me to go out and work in the orchard, I lay on my mat and didn't get up. When he told me to do something, I did as he said. Reports of the festivities and celebrations throughout the country, and of the grand military parade in Jerusalem, reached me from people who came to visit Mehmet Effendi, but none of that touched me at all. Until one day Luna came to the packing shed while Obadiah was away in Jaffa on business, and signaled to me with her hands and eyes to get up and follow her. I obeyed and went up the stone steps above the pool, and she led me to Mehmet Effendi's bedroom. The old man was lying on the floor in his undergarments, his big paunch rising and falling slowly, a sign that he was still alive. Beside him on the floor lay his old wife, caressing his face with her hands, her eyes dripping tears. Luna and I picked up the old man by the armpits and lifted his fat body onto the bed. His wife hastily covered his nakedness with a blanket, and I went down to saddle the donkey and ride off to Jaffa for the English doctor. Close to noon I brought him back in a rented carriage, and he examined Mehmet Effendi for a long time, prescribed medicines, spoke to the old man, and forced him to answer. With great effort and much internal pain the old man started speaking broken words. Then the doctor nodded his head as a sign that he was satisfied, and patted Mehmet Effendi on the shoulder. When he turned to leave, he took me by the arm and led me to the porch, where he told me that the Turk's fate was sealed. He had been stricken with an incurable paralysis, and his travails were liable to last a long time.

In the afternoon Obadiah came back from town, and I told him what had happened. He went out to the clearing opposite the porch, next to the pool, and gestured to Luna from afar to join him. The two of them quickly went deep into the orchard and vanished among the trees.

On the third day of Mehmet Effendi's illness his condition improved, and he asked for me to be called to his room. When I came in, he motioned to his wife to leave, signaled me to approach his bed, and spoke with me for a long while. He said that his days were drawing to a close and that he would like to be returned to the place of his birth, Izmir, to be buried there. He asked me to go to Jerusalem and Jaffa to find a Jewish buyer for his orchard. The Jews pay good prices, he said, and I knew many orchard-owners and had contacts among my people. He also made me swear that if he died before the orchard was sold, I would take care of having his bones shipped to Izmir and would divide the money equally between his wife and Luna, for each to do with as she willed.

I told him that the doctor would cure him of his ailment and that he should not speak of the day of his death. Mehmet Effendi waved his hand impatiently, as if to tell me not to talk nonsense. But during the succeeding days his conditon really did improve, and he ate his meals like a completely healthy man. He only couldn't move from his bed. And when more than a week had passed, he again urged me to go and find a buyer for his orchard. Seeing him fully conscious and clear-minded and firm in his resolve, I no longer saw any point in opposing him. An owner of property may do with his property what he wishes. I therefore started preparing myself for the journey, and when I was ready, I took my leave of Mehmet Effendi and he again reminded me of the oath I had sworn.

First I went to Jerusalem. I had stayed in the Holy City only once before, soon after my arrival in the land of Israel, and I remember how it had grieved me to see my brothers debased by living on charity, existing on donations and sending messages to the Diaspora, to suck its blood, like the most contemptible of men. That visit left me with mixed memories of sorrow and yearning. It did not escape me that a different kind of life was possible in Jerusalem, a life perhaps more beautiful and more elevated than in any other orchard in the world.

Now I entered the city by train, through the German Colony where houses of splendid stone rested in the shade of trees, and the entire sight bespoke glory. It was painful to compare it to the damp dark hovels in which tubercular Jews were crammed together in the Old City. My eyes immediately lit up on seeing a big attractive notice stuck to the wall of the train station, bearing the following message: "The most pleasant and orderly hotel is the Warshawsky Hotel. Run according to the rules of hygiene, baths, showers, sewerage, and electric light. The windows open upon historic sites. Delightful garden. Healthful European dishes. We use only spring water, brought by pipes. Prompt and precise service — telephone and bus service. Guests are met by hotel staff and in buses."

And indeed I reached the hotel by bus No. 94 and took a pleasant room, and for a moment almost became human again. I almost forgot the reason for my coming here. But the moments of intoxication didn't last long. For it was a stranger's money that had paid for my journey here, and with a stranger's money I was paying my board. I thus hastened to make contacts and connections among public men and men of affairs.

I spent three days in Jerusalem, and my efforts were all in vain. It seemed that people who wanted to buy an orchard lived not in Jerusalem but rather in Jaffa, close to our place. Everyone I consulted told me it might take ages until the fruit business returned to pre-war conditions. And if I did happen to meet someone interested in an orchard, it turned out that his interest was in speculation, not in agriculture.

Thus at the end of three days I made up my mind to return to Jaffa, and on the fourth day I set out.

In Jaffa I had no need of a hotel. I spent the nights in the packing shed, and every morning, at dawn, I harnessed the donkey and drove to the city of Jaffa, where I spent the day in the vicinity of the port and the offices and companies that in those days were springing up like mushrooms — public companies and private companies, some intent on settling the land of Israel and some out for prey and profit.

6 A Meeting at a Dying Man's Bedside

From my negotiations with people I discovered that if anyone did want to buy an orchard — this was the end of 1919 — then what they wanted was a healthy orchard, one young and abundant in yield. Mehmet Effendi's stuffed mummies were known to most of the veteran settlers in our area and aroused little enthusiasm among them, unless they had an eye toward uprooting and speculation. And this I didn't want. Some kind of stubbornness from my previous life made me cling to the thought that I'd find someone who would try to cure this orchard by thinning out its trees and planting new ones. I had promised myself that if I found a Jew with a mind for orchardry, I would stand by him with guidance and advice, even if my status in the orchard remained what it was now — that of a sick parasite who slept on a mat in the packing shed. From there, too, from the mat, I would still be able to do great things. So I boasted to myself, sometimes wholeheartedly believing in my strength and sometimes doubting, but wanting with all my might.

That being the case, I gave up hoping for results from the company offices and stopped following up offers by land-speculators. Instead, I tried to make a connection with one of the Jewish immigrants coming in by ship to Jaffa port, especially those who wanted to tour the country first, with money in their pockets and the intention of putting down roots in the land of our fathers. In order to meet these people before they fell into the hands of the many kinds of speculators, swindlers, and tempters, I needed advance knowledge of the day an immigrant ship was due to arrive, and I saw the best thing I could do then was to watch them coming in by boats from the ship, follow them on their way to their hotel, and, out of the mass of human visages, decide on a face that appealed to me.

To get reliable information about the ships, all I had to do was have a chat with Mahmoud Unbarjee, who ran practically everything in and around the port. The moment I heard something definite from him, I would climb up the hill behind the Kishla. There, in the company of boatmen and sailors, I would sit in the coffeehouse beside the Ramazan cannon, sip from my cup, and watch for the ship's arrival. When the boatmen went down to the sea to bring in the passengers, I would go down with them and stand on the pier to look over the new people.

As I say, this method seemed the best designed for my needs, but in truth I had no way of knowing if I was doing well in trying it this way or whether I was just wasting my time, thus disappointing the last hope of a man on the verge of death. Mehmet Effendi's condition affected me deeply, and with all my might I wanted to be of use to him and to make sure that, before his death, he could know that he had received a good price, that his wife and daughter were protected from the ravages of time, and also that I would be in a position to get him to Izmir while he yet lived.

Until my riddle finally solved itself I had no way of guessing how well I had done in choosing the method I have just described. A man sitting on top of a hill, sipping coffee above Jaffa port — well, his nostrils fill with fleshy odors and his eyes are awash in a dark greenness, and it is impossible for him to know what is happening out at sea, on the deck of a ship several miles away. And what I found out days, years, later — that I shall tell now.

A ship with two smokestacks made its way on the sea, approaching the shore of Jaffa. What it was carrying in its hold, I don't remember. It was probably bringing wooden planks from Rumania, and coal, canned food, and some motors for the new wells they had started drilling here. But I know that on its upper deck, among the first-class passengers, there sat at that moment the man I had been waiting and praying for. He was dressed most elegantly, though he came from the lands of war, the war that had ended only a year before; and apart from being elegantly dressed, his face was young and handsome, the face of a young man of about twenty-two, whose world had not been despoiled or his soul stricken by injuries. He was solidly built, with a sharp eye and an open heart, ready to see and accept what life had to offer of pleasure and labor and conquest. Much later he told me that while the ship was approaching Jaffa, he was unable to sleep at night and did not eat all day because of his inner turmoil. He was an orphan, and in thus coming to the land of Israel he was fulfilling the last wishes of his parents, who all their lives had been preparing to go to the land of Israel, though their prayer had not been answered. They had both died in an epidemic that had devastated the population of their city during the war. Now, in possession of all their wealth, gold, and precious stones and jewellery, he was fulfilling their command to him, his heart weeping for what was irretrievable. Much later he also told me that they had taught him the holy tongue since his childhood, and so he was well-versed in our books, his days in the Diaspora being like a corridor through which he would enter the vestibule. At the same time he confessed to me that during those last two or three days aboard ship he had not thought of the Western Wall, or of the site of the Temple, or of all the other spiritual things of which his soul had been full in the Diaspora, but had mused and daydreamed, his mind circling around one sole goal. He was young, ripe for doing deeds, and yearning for his bride — and this bride, the one proclaimed by a heavenly voice saying, This woman is for this man — he saw her with the eyes of his soul. She appeared before him as if alive, with her russet hair, her brown eyes, her stature, and her limbs; there was not the tiniest detail of her appearance that this young man did not see. She arose and stood before him as if alive, and he even heard her voice speaking to him of what his heart wanted to hear.

He told me about all this much later, as I say. As for me, the moment I saw him sitting in the boat and then getting up to climb the steps to the pier, I knew immediately that here was the man I had been waiting for ever since Mehmet Effendi had commanded me to sell his orchard. I don't know how to explain why I felt so confident that I had really found what I was looking for. Perhaps it was the candor of his face, the face of an honest and vigorous man who had no crookedness in him, that charmed me. And perhaps deeper inner forces were at work, forces of which I have no knowledge.

At any rate, I marched forward, offered him my hand, and bade him welcome. His handshake reinforced my original feeling on seeing his face: it was the sincere handshake of a man who trusts others and is open to forging an alliance. In such things the heart does not err. Unfortunate the man whose heart does not know how to read in this language!

He greeted me in return and, lightly grasping my shoulder, asked if I was one of the committee receiving arrivals from the lands of the Diaspora. I introduced myself by name and told him I was not a member of any committee but was interested in meeting a man of Israel who had come to establish a home in our country.

With the help of the above-mentioned Mahmoud Unbarjee, we concluded my new acquaintance's business in customs and all the other offices in several hours, and then we went into the restaurant of a Jewish hotel, not far from the Seraia, and sat down to dine. An hour or two before sunset my acquaintance wanted to go for a walk in the city, and I took him to the narrow streets that climbed the cliff. He walked beside me excited and happy, stopping at every step, touching the stones of the houses, filling his lungs with the nauseating smells of frying oil, of mutton roasting with onions and tomatoes and spiced with garlic and peppers, and his face glowed as if he had attained to a revelation of the Divine Presence. I laughed, and he laughed with me. And thus we walked for about two hours, while shopkeepers accompanied us with shouts, inviting us to see their wares, and wanton girls peeped out at us through window lattices, calling to us with digusting cries, and I laughed and he laughed with me.

At dark I left him at his hotel and we agreed to meet the next day, at daybreak. On my return to the orchard I went up to Mehmet Effendi's room and without any hesitation — although I had nothing final at all to go on — told him that our affair was proceeding well and that I hoped and believed the right buyer had been found.

I will not draw out the story. In the morning I told my acquaintance what I had to offer, without concealing a thing. He heard from me that the orchard was old and infected; that much work had to be done, but the earth was good, the well deep and clean, and the house a six-room mansion with stables and storage sheds and an attic in addition, and the pool strong and whole.

But after describing the property to him and stating the

price and telling him it was not too high — in fact, possibly a real bargain — after all this I informed him that I would not sell him the property unless he first made a tour of the country, from Jaffa and Tel Aviv to the Sharon and the Galilee and Jerusalem, so that he could see and hear what others had to offer. Only if after this survey he still inclined to my proposal would I be willing to draw up a sales agreement.

Again he laughed and said: But you're not going to hide the orchard from me, my friend. Before I take your advice and go look around the country, will you not agree to show me the property you want me to make my own?

So we rented a carriage and drove to the orchard, and before going up to the room where Mehmet Effendi lay sick in his bed, we walked around among the trees for close to an hour. There was not a living soul to be seen all around. I don't know where Obadiah was that day, but search as I might I could not find him. I showed the man the packing shed, but didn't tell him it was my home. I believed that if he saw my situation he might well doubt the reliability of what he had heard from me. Later, I said to myself, I'll tell him the whole story of my life, and if he wants my advice, I will hire myself into his service.

The place is big and beautiful and exhilarating, said my acquaintance. Do you believe a man could bring it back to life and see the reward of his labor?

I guarantee that on my honor, I told him. Go to the members of the Growers' Association and ask them. Go to anyone who knows about orchards. They'll tell you. On my honor I guarantee it to you.

Well, then, shall we have a talk with the owner of the orchard? he said.

I left him on the veranda and went into the sick man's room to inform him of our arrival. Then I immediately returned and invited my acquaintance to come into the room. The guest sat on the chair, and I stood at the head of the bed and acted as interpreter.

The guest asked his questions politely and Mehmet Effendi answered in a weak voice, but with the dignity worthy of his station. And since he saw before him a well-mannered man who knew how to conduct himself in conversation without hasty questioning or contemptible suspicions, as are displayed by many people during negotiations over a deal, Mehmet Effendi ordered me to call his wife, and when she came he told her in their language to bring coffee and fruits and cakes. And to me he said that indeed he could see that I had brought a decent buyer.

After a short while Luna came into the room, carrying a copper tray with little cups of coffee on it and various kinds of sweetmeats.

At that moment the guest looked up and saw Luna. And when he saw her, he leapt up from his seat. The action of a European gentleman, I said to myself. When they see a woman, they leap up from their seat.

But I was mistaken.

When he got up from his seat, a cry escaped from his mouth and he immediately collapsed in a swoon.

7 The Death of Mehmet Effendi. Uprooting and New Planting

When the guest fell down in a swoon, Luna went out of the room after putting the tray with the delicacies on the table. Moments later Mehmet Effendi's wife came in, alarmed, and together we sat our guest up on the chair and splashed water on him until he opened his eyes.

Mehmet Effendi said: You are tired from the journey by ship, and your heart is weak.

The guest said: Forgive me. I blacked out for a moment. It's nothing.

Mehmet Effendi said: Return to your hotel and rest for two or three days, and then we shall discuss our affair again.

The guest said: I will not return to my hotel unless you give me your hand on the conclusion of this deal, at a good and propitious hour.

Mehmet Effendi said: Son, you are being hasty, and possibly you will regret it later.

The guest said: I will not move from here, even if you double the price of the orchard.

Mehmet Effendi laughed a thin laugh and said to me in Arabic: You've brought a madman to my house. What does he want?

I said to him: Perhaps he isn't mad. And as for what he wants, you just heard him tell you.

Mehmet Effendi said: Son, are you mad?

The guest said: If I tell you what is in my heart at this moment, you will have no doubt that I'm completely mad.

Mehmet Effendi said: Speak, then.

The guest said: I have heard that, among the Muslims, when a man marries a woman he pays her parents a dowry. I want to marry your daughter, even though I'm a Jew and she's a Muslim. State her price.

Mehmet Effendi beckoned him to approach his bedside. The guest got up from his seat and leaned over the old man. Mehmet

Effendi took the end of the guest's mustache between the thumb and forefinger of his hand, pulled it affectionately, and looked into his eyes for a short while.

She is not my daughter, and she was not born a Muslim. She comes from a highly reputed family. Her father was like a as a Jew. He was murdered by his Arab neighbors. If you want to marry o me, and he wher, she is yours. The orchard and the daughter for the one price.

The guest bent down and kissed the old man's hand. Mehmet Effendi placed his other hand on the guest's head and said to him: May God bless this mating.

At that moment there was a sound of feet stamping in the doorway. We turned to see who was coming in, and there was Obadiah standing on the threshold.

Ho, Abdullah, said Mehmet Effendi, here is your new master. Say a courteous word to him, because from now on he is owner of the orchard.

The guest got up from the bedside and turned to Obadiah, and the two stood there looking at each other.

At first we thought that their silence was the silence of politeness. But as it became prolonged, to a minute, then two, then three and four, I began noticing that Obadiah was smiling impudently, while the guest's hands were trembling and a pallor was spreading over his face. I feared he would faint again, and I went up and pushed the chair under him. But he did not sit down. He opened his mouth and spoke:

Are you not my brother Obadiah?

And Obadiah, who had not stopped smiling that cold smile, said: I may be your brother, Daniel.

Daniel said: And are you not glad to see me?

Obadiah said: I may be glad and I may not be glad.

Daniel said: Give me your hand.

They reached out their hands to each other and fell upon each other's neck and stood there in an embrace for a long time, hiding their faces in each other's shoulder, while Mehmet Effendi and I looked on in silent amazement.

That was how it happened; I have not added or subtracted a thing. Someone born yesterday may be surprised at the convolutions of fate. But one with gray hair sprouting in his mustache knows that in this world there have been greater wonders, and even mysterious things like this are not astonishing.

That day Daniel returned to his hotel in Jaffa and I went with him, and when we reached Jaffa and entered his hotel room, I said to him: I will not draw up the deed until you solve two riddles for me. One — why did you cry out and faint when you saw Luna? And the other — Obadiah.

And on that occasion I heard from him what I have already narrated of Obadiah's beginnings. But from what Obadiah had told me during the seven years we had already spent together, I knew a lot more than Daniel now said. I immediately informed him that they were sons of the same father but not of the same mother, and so forth. Daniel was very agitated. Then I demanded the answer to the first riddle, and he replied with the story I have already mentioned: the figure of Luna was the one that had appeared to him in his visions on board the ship; she was the girl he had dreamed of in every detail, the living likeness, with no difference between them except that the first had appeared to him in a dream and the second was the answer to the dream. And when he told me that in his dream Luna had spoken to him and had told him of the things his heart longed to hear, I revealed to him that Luna was dumb. Daniel said, without any doubt: From the day I marry her, she'll to speak to me. You'll see. She'll be cured.

At the end of that year we drew up and signed the sales agreement, which was then officially registered at the Land Office as the law prescribed. And all that time Mehmet Effendi's health held out, with no change either for better or for worse. On the day of Daniel and Luna's wedding, we picked up his bed and carried it to the veranda, so he could participate in the celebration. On the bridegroom's side I brought some Jewish growers from the area, and on the bride's side some of the old Turk's acquaintances came. Obadiah was with us, too, sitting with some boatmen from the port. Ali Khamis sat at their head, because no celebration took place among the Arabs of Jaffa without the head boatman.

And if I say I saw glances stealing from Luna's eyes to Obadiah's, I will be saying nothing that is not reasonable to suppose and self-evident.

Two days after the wedding, Mehmet Effendi lost consciousness, and on the third day he died. I kept my vow, and with Unbarjee's help we bought a coffin of strong tin; the body was placed in it and the cover welded on, and after some time a ship was located to take the coffin and the old man's wife, too, to Izmir. And thus I found myself released from my vow.

Luna allowed the old woman to cry on her shoulder, but from her own eyes not one tear fell, not when Mehmet Effendi died and not when she parted from her foster mother. And thus began our new life in the orchard.

I again became the expert adviser, running the affairs of the orchard, and Obadiah remained in his position, overseeing the workers and helping me. Daniel brought several good builders, and by the packing shed they erected a special wing, made of stone and equipped with everything a man needs in his dwelling — a sink for water and a toilet, furniture and a bed — and once more Obadiah no longer slept on a mat.

At Daniel's special request we left several clusters of dense plantings around the house. He wanted to preserve the sights and landscapes to which Luna had grown accustomed. Nor did we uproot lemons or pomegranates or figs. But each planting season we reshaped the face of the orchard, according to what was necessary by modern rules and practices; we took care to grow the Shamuti strain — since its discovery in Selim Ayub's orchard, near Tabitha's grave, no better strain had been found or one more favored by buyers overseas. And because we were not pressed financially, the orchard had a chance to arise from the dust, and after several years it was possible to say of it what is written in our books: "And he shall be like a tree planted by the rivers of water, that bringeth forth fruit in his season, and his leaf shall not wither."

And together with this orchard, even though it was not mine, I also arose from the dust. Though I never again became what I had been, and only some of my wounds healed. For me, too, Daniel had a small wing built, next to Obadiah's room, and in the course of time I moved into the big house above the pool, as I shall relate further on. But, as I say, I never returned to my former self. On the other hand, there again awoke in me desires that had slumbered since my youth, and I started collecting books and journals to take to my room and read in the evenings. After 1915 I never fell asleep before midnight, and even then my sleep was troubled and bad dreams visited me.

But in the orchard everything went well, and if one can speak of repair in a person's life, then this is the place to speak of it, and I am the person.

Not so Daniel's life.

8 Better and Better

In October of 1924 we finished the graftings in our last section of plantings, thus concluding the work of renewing the orchard. Those trees, which we grafted in 1924, were to start yielding in 1929, and from then on the whole orchard would be clear profit. That year, 1924, Luna became pregnant and in June of 1925 her son was born; and in the year the section mentioned above started yielding fruit — in 1929 — the great pogrom broke out, like the one in 1921 but even worse. This time Obadiah's friends, the boatmen from the port, joined the rioters, and many Jews were slaughtered and killed in cruel and ugly ways; childhood friends turned traitors, and Arabs who had had dealings of trade and friendship with their Jewish neighbors supported the rioters and joined in the looting, shedding blood with knives and revolvers. But there were also other cases, in which Arab neighbors came out to defend Jews. Daniel's orchard was not broken into by any stranger, and in the vicinity of our house not one human hair was touched. That summer, and also in the autumn of that year, Obadiah hardly slept one night in his room in the orchard. As to whether he had a hand in the activities of his boatmen friends, I must say I don't know. But there is reason to suppose that even if he did make an alliance with them, he surely intervened with them on the orchard's behalf, and precisely because he was involved in criminal deeds, he was able to protect us and prevent us from falling with the fallen.

That year Luna's son was about four, and there is reason to suppose that it was because of him that Obadiah protected us. I think that Obadiah in his stupidity believed the child was his; the truth will never be known, because it cannot be known. At any rate, when I say these terrible things now, I cannot hurt any living soul. Today, some thirty years after the events described here, no one remains to be sorry about them. No one but me.

Again I have anticipated, and I now return to the things as they happened. Between 1924 and 1929 we did excellent business, and I have never seen a man handle his business so wisely as Daniel. On whatever had to do with agriculture or the agronomy of the orchard he would accept my advice without the slightest hesitation. But he never consulted me on matters of commerce, such as delivery dates, the characters of the agents, or the tricks of shipmasters, merchants in London and in other places. That was wise of him. It was not for me, the destroyed failure, to teach wisdom to a successful man.

He devoted himself to his business with all his heart and soul, with a fervor such as we had seen only in our fathers' fathers, when they served their God with faith and died for the sanctity of the Name when that became necessary. He knew neither day nor night, neither meal time nor resting time, neither Sabbath nor holiday; whenever the orchard needed him, there he was, ready and willing. And there is no other way to do one's work — anyone who lacks such dedication is like the priest of a temple in which there is not perfect faith. Woe to that temple, and woe to its priests.

Yet there was another reason for the avidity with which Daniel served his orchard, and that was his love for Luna. Today I know that from his very first moment with us he was not ignorant of what had been happening before his arrival and continued to go on afterwards. Daniel, too, tended to think there were two Lunas, not one. But he could never know. And in order to drown the pain, and because he could not live without Luna, he devoted himself to the only thing he could conquer completely— the orchard. I am probably not exaggerating when I say that, for Daniel, Luna and the orchard were one. Possibly I've said something stupid. At any rate, this is as far as my understanding goes, no higher.

The truth is that after 1915 I never became quite healthy again. I'm referring to mental balance. I have already told how a total blackness came over me close to the disaster; but after that it seemed that I was cured. From time to time I would fall from a man's degree to that of a child, and there were hours and days when people left me alone until the trouble passed. During those bad hours I found release in a childish thing, an old habit from my school days: I wrote things down in a diary. It is from those notes that I am now compiling this story. Since the diary was written during those bad hours, there may well be some totally stupid things in it. But I have no other source to draw from. And for this reason my opinions ought to be doubted — though the facts, at least, need not be questioned, I hope.

Moreover, Daniel would come to my room and sit up with me, sometimes all night long, and converse with me at length, especially during those bad days when part of my reason was in hiding, while the other part became sharper than ever and in a kind of heightened alertness empowered me to register things and speak words that were not mine at all; thus almost all I know about the lives of Daniel and Luna and Obadiah I heard during those twisted hours, which were either the hiding of the Presence or else its special revelation.

Also in my diary are some instructive figures, which may be of some use to anyone who decides to write the history of orchardry in this country. In that last section of the orchard where we finished the graftings in 1924, we did not plant the trees two meters apart, as the Arabs did, or five meters apart, as did the more daring and learned of the Jewish growers. Daniel and I took an original step and planted the trees seven meters apart. Nowadays this is no innovation, and everybody knows what needs to be known. But we were the first. And in our battles against tree diseases we also introduced innovations. Daniel would bring back different kinds of remedies from his trips abroad, remedies such as had not been known in this country before. But if I tell all, the space I have will not suffice.

When Daniel traveled abroad on business, Luna and Obadiah made no secret of their behavior, not even from the orchard workers. But on his return, Daniel never asked me about this and never made me a spy or an informer. Yet those nights, when he spoke to me with that extreme candor, I confessed to him my puzzlement, and the answer he gave me is written down in my diary.

I have told you, said Daniel, that when I was on the ship coming to the land of Israel, I saw Luna in a dream, and I have not the slightest doubt that she is the woman intended for me by heaven. And if there is difficulty in this, or even something higher than custom and lower than what is customary, there is no way for me not to accept this judgment. She is my wife, and this is how things are between us, and I have to accept it. And I will tell you one more thing: had my brother not run off from my father's house, would he not have received his share of the inheritance? And had he arrived in the land of Israel with money, would he not have been able to buy the orchard and Luna from Mehmet Effendi, exactly as I did? And is it not possible that he, too, dreamed of all these things, and his prayer was not answered?

I didn't restrain myself. What Daniel had said was despicable, and I could not square it with human nature; Daniel's excessive righteousness seemed to me like a contortion of the soul, a disease of the mind. So I said to him: Obadiah has never put his mind to the orchard any more than he has needed to at any given moment, for his own profit; and he has never dreamed of Luna — he has only quenched his momentary lust with her, the lust of a male for a female.

Daniel laughed bitterly and said: That you cannot know.

If Luna was meant for you by heaven, I pressed him mercilessly, why hasn't she been cured of her disease? Why doesn't she speak to you as you were shown in the dream?

She'll speak, said Daniel. The time hasn't come yet. But when that day comes, she'll speak.

What day will that be? I asked angrily.

Maybe the day I die, said Daniel.

I spat on the floor and said: They won't see that day, neither she nor Obadiah.

Daniel looked at me like one who knows something concealed from other mortals, and we did not speak.

One night Daniel came to me and we talked, and we both knew that on the other side of the wall, in Obadiah's room, Luna was with Obadiah. But we said not a word about that. At first we spoke about orchard affairs, and afterwards Daniel told me some things about his childhood in his father's house. Suddenly he stopped, grasped my hand firmly, and said: Did you hear?

I strained my ears and heard neither voice nor sound.

I don't hear a thing, I said.

Daniel released my hand, lit a cigarette, and remained silent. After a moment he whispered again: Now do you hear?

This time, too, I heard nothing. And there really was nothing to hear. All around us, the night was still like a grave.

Then Daniel's lips mumbled some words, and I heard him

say: She's speaking to him. She's speaking.

I strained my ears with all my might, and I was certain there was no speaking to be heard beyond the wall. But Daniel whispered again: She's speaking to him. To me she has never spoken.

Then I saw tears roll from his eyes, and I turned my face to the wall.

9 They Move to Tel Aviv and I — to the Orchard House

In 1930 — the year Luna and the brothers and Luna's son moved to Tel Aviv — several things that had been hanging vaguely in the air fell into place and took shape. The brothers had devised a kind of division of labor: Obadiah took care of the business connected with the port, negotiating with the customs police, distributing bribes to officials, and supervising the loading of the fruit vessels being sent abroad; I oversaw the orchard and the workers in it; and Daniel devoted himself to the trading side. He conducted correspondence with brokers abroad, and from time to time he sailed to them; he also handled all the monetary affairs. From this arrangement it was clear that the brothers had divided the ownership of the orchard equally between themselves, and I remained what I had been at the beginning, when Mehmet Effendi was still alive. I no longer had an orchard of my own, but the confidence Daniel placed in me was sufficient to give me a will to work and to live.

That year Luna's son was about five, and I could already see signs of his uniqueness. Once, when he was hanging around the Arab cooking women in his mother's kitchen, he heard them say that two hens had to be killed for dinner. Right away he ran down to the yard and several minutes later returned to the kitchen, holding two hens with their heads pulled off. The cooks screamed with terror and awe, and Luna's son took obvious delight in both the terror he had aroused in them and the admiration that gazed out of their dumb eyes. Another time I saw him waiting in ambush for a hare that was wandering around the bushes in the flowerbeds, and saw him suddenly throw himself upon it and trap it. Then he held it by the hind legs and started smashing its head against a tree trunk until it stopped fluttering. He would spend the bulk of the day with the Arab workers in the orchard and taught himself to speak their perverted language; and once he came to me and showed me what he had in his hand — an arum flower, of the species that grows a thick black pistil from the navel of its calyx.

You know what this is? he said to me. And without waiting for my answer, he repeated what he had heard from the workers: That's a *zib-el-abed.* That is, a Negro's penis. I scolded him, and he looked at me and laughed.

I told Daniel what I had seen in Luna's son. He answered that he had already given the matter some thought, and next year, when the boy would start going to school, they were going to move from the orchard to live in Tel Aviv. He had already ordered an apartment on Rothschild Boulevard and had made an advance payment to an agent in the city and would soon have an automobile.

And you'll take charge of the orchard house, said Daniel, and if you want to, you'll get yourself a wife and delight in your life.

And Obadiah? I asked.

Obadiah will move with us, replied Daniel.

And he'll wear that red tarboosh of his in Tel Aviv? I wanted to know. After the pogrom of 1929, the people in Tel Aviv might stone him if they see him walking around in that tarboosh.

That's up to him, said Daniel. But I know my brother, I think he'll remove the tarboosh when he's in Tel Aviv and put it on again when he's in Jaffa.

Good thinking, I answered him. You really do know your brother.

And that was how it was. From their first day in Tel Aviv, Obadiah removed the tarboosh from his head, but in Jaffa he took care to wear it. In Tel Aviv he spoke to people in Hebrew, and in Jaffa — Arabic. And however much he changed, this way and that, he remained fixed to his own nature, as the French say. And Daniel treated him with a strange affection, showering him with gifts and presents. I never forgave Daniel this, God forgive me.

When I found myself alone in the orchard house with the key in my possession, I went up the steps above the pool and stayed on the threshold a long time, as if trying to hear if there was anyone in the house, listening for the sound of shuffling feet or a drawer falling, or an armchair being drawn along the floor, or any of those sounds of a house that fill a listener outside with envy for its inhabitants and pity for himself. And since I heard no sound, one might think I felt neither envy for others nor pity for myself. But no. A kind of malignant sadness crept and crawled into me, into my heart, spreading outwards and increasing from day to day. This sorrow didn't leave me all the time I lived there, for more than twenty years.

When I put the key in the keyhole and opened the door, I entered the same house to which Mehmet Effendi had taken me seventeen years earlier, when he asked me to act as instructor to his Abdullah. Covers of white cloth, sewn like stuffings of a sofa and armchairs, covered all the seats in the house, those seats upholstered in red velvet and Damascus fabric embroidered with gold; the covers were removed only to clean the dust that had gathered between them and the splendid upholstery. On the wall hung a picture of Mehmet Effendi and his wife on their wedding day, as well as a picture of their relatives wearing swords and ammunition belts. A big bouquet of colored paper flowers in a copper vase stood on a Damascene cabinet made of Cretan wood and inlaid with shell engravings. A heavy kerosene lamp hung from the ceiling on chains of copper cast in the shapes of flowers and branches tangled in each other, with a kerosene container made of porcelain decorated with painted flowers and a shade of opaque white glass surrounding them all, like the headdress of an esteemed matron. The dimness in the room was broken by strips of light that penetrated between the two parts of each of the six shutters, and specks of gold floated in the strips of light, hanging on nothing, motionless.

Eh, I said to myself aloud, as was my custom. And when I got no response, I said: Oh well.

I locked the door behind me, and without opening any of the windows I carefully sat down on one of the armchairs covered with white cloth, taking care not to crease it, as if the lady of the house, the old wife of the dead Turk, were sitting before me. And as though of their own accord, my thoughts wandered from the place where I was sitting to the places outside, around me.

That there had been no change in the arrangement and furniture of the house, I could understand. Luna had been used to it from her youth, and her husband had not brought any furniture with him when he came to our country. Nevertheless I stubbornly followed up a thought that was bothering me: outside, in the orchard, Daniel had wrought far-reaching changes. One could almost say that he had changed the entire landscape all around, while inside the house he had made no mark of his own. Even the felt slippers, which people from overseas were accustomed to wearing when they walked on the polished wooden floors of their homes, even those he had exchanged for wooden clogs, which Luna had pushed under his feet, the same clogs Mehmet Effendi had stumbled around in all the days of his life.

Oh well, I said again, aloud, into the dimness of the room.

From outside, from the depths of the orchard, there occasionally came into the room the sound of one of the Arab workers calling out, and afterwards a prolonged silence. Was I supposed to feel afraid? On more than one occasion in my life I had found myself alone, a single Jew in a sea of Arabs, and I had not been afraid. Why then should I fear now? Perhaps because this very place, this house and this orchard, had already been bought by Jews and made into Jewish soil and had now suddenly been abandoned, as it were, as if somewhere an announcement had proclaimed that all this was now no man's land.

Eh, I said, dismissing my thoughts. Get up, man. Get up and do something.

So I got up and went to the kitchen and poured some water into the kettle and put it on the stove and lit a fire, and from my pocket I took out a pita bread, broke off a piece, dipped it in some salt that was on the table, and put it in my mouth. Oh well.

10 The Celebration and What the Papers Wrote About It

Several days after they all moved to Tel Aviv, Daniel came and spent the night with me at the orchard house. Already? So soon? I said to myself, but I asked no questions.

That night we made plans for innovations in the orchard. We decided to install a modern pump and to see what could be done about deepening the well, so that it would provide us with all the water we needed. And, in fact, several months later the new pump, packed and greased, arrived by ship. It weighed eleven tons and arrived in parts packed in six crates. We took the crates to the packing shed and stored them under the roof. Following the specifications we had received from Germany, we began pouring concrete foundations and fixing iron pegs, bolts and nuts, and all the other apparatus of the pump. While this work went on, everyone returned to the orchard again except Luna, who didn't even bother to come and take a look at the equipment and the bustle. More than anyone, Luna's son was enthralled by the work of erecting the pump, and though he was but a boy, a little more than six years old, he found a way to take part in all the various jobs, displaying an unbelievably discriminating eye for the parts and qualities of the machine. Although I risk being suspected of making this up, I would say that the boy understood the details of assembly no less than the Arab mechanic who had been sent by the machine company's agent and who was practically useless in any case.

After completing our preparations, assembling the engine, starting it up for a trial run, and seeing that it worked well, a kind of celebration or housewarming was clearly in order. Daniel felt so, too, and we set a day and an hour and sent invitations, by messenger and by mail, to growers of our acquaintance and to some English officials from the Department of Agriculture, to the head boatman, to Unbarjee, and to the chief of the customs police and other such notables.

I took Luna's son with me to Jaffa, where we went to the

shops in Bustrus Street and bought Japanese paper lanterns and colored candles and different kinds of paper chains, and on returning to the orchard we both set to work. Several hours later the pool was decorated with colored pennants, and among the posts of the veranda we had stretched wires and hung the paper lanterns on them and fixed the candles inside them, to be lit at sunset when the guests would come out of the bar and gather on the veranda, to be served sweetmeats and drinks and various delicacies. Servants from the Tel Aviv house came to prepare the foods, with an additional complement of the wives of the orchard workers. Only Luna did not appear there all day, but in the afternoon she came, at about the time the guests began to arrive. She was most elegantly dressed; but all her elegance seemed to be hanging upon her by accident, her entire being bespeaking impatient anticipation for the moment when she would shed all these trappings of European ladies and return to her simple cloth garments or to her nakedness; as I've already said, Luna walked around in clothes the way a naked woman walks.

After the engine was started and the place filled with the sound of its mighty snorting pumping, all the guests clapped, and one of the English officials made a speech in Arabic and again everyone clapped, and then Daniel announced that he was inviting his guests onto the veranda, to sit down at the tables. He gave Luna his arm, and the two of them led the guests out and climbed the steps above the pool, followed by some thirty men and women dressed in their best clothes. And I brought up the rear with Luna's son, watching to see what impression our decorations would make on the guests. From the expressions on some of their faces we saw that they were pleased with us.

A few days later nearly all the newspapers wrote about our celebration and praised the development that Jewish growers were bringing to the country. But the "Do'ar Ha-yom" wrote that it was a scandal, because the English official had spoken Arabic, thus hinting as to which of the two nations he sympathized with. Furthermore, the paper continued, the owner of the orchard should have protested vigorously about this; since he hadn't protested, there had to be something behind it.

Daniel flushed on reading these slanderous words, and I said to him it was not the language spoken by the English official that would determine the facts in this country, but the deeds done by Daniel and his like. Obadiah kept silent, but there was a malicious smile in his eyes. Luna also kept silent, naturally. After all, she was dumb; but it was also possible that she had not read what was written in the newspapers. I showed Luna's son Daniel's name printed in the newspaper, and he was pleased.

That celebration wrought a change in the lives of the orchard's owners. Having seen how attractive the place was when it was buzzing with people, gaily decorated and inspiring merriment in all who came there, they made it a rule to go there every Sabbath day. They would pack food into their car, and some of their friends would also come, some in their own cars, some in rented cars, and from morning till evening the orchard would be like a festival place, as if a wedding were being held there, or a circumcision. And when I saw that the custom had become a rule, I bought a gramophone in Tel Aviv and several records of dances and Russian songs and other songs, and there was no end to the guests' delight, and everyone praised me for my good taste.

When the members of the family were not to come one Sabbath, they made it their custom to invite me to their table in Tel Aviv, on the Sabbath Eve, and there I saw several strange things.

Their apartment in Tel Aviv was not as spacious as the house in the orchard, even though there, too, they had six rooms; but the rooms were low, small, and cramped around a narrow corridor, where if you wanted to stretch your bones and spread out your arms you would bump into the walls and hurt your fingers.

Still, Daniel brought new furniture from Europe and the house glinted with the gleam of the smooth wood, and one could delight in the colors of the upholstery, which there was not covered with white cloth.

And the strangest thing I saw was this: when it grew dark, on Sabbath Eve, Luna lit candles in the silver candlesticks that stood at the center of the dining table. And immediately afterwards we started eating. She did not make the benediction over the candles, because she was dumb, and also because she lit them as one who has learned by rote. For it was Daniel who had told her to do so. The Sabbath candlesticks were his mother's, among the few articles he had brought with him from Russia. At the orchard house he had not bothered about lighting them. But there, in his Tel Aviv house, he thought differently.

And so we sat at the Sabbath table, with Sabbath candles alight even though no blessing had been spoken over them, and around the table — two Jews, one half-breed with a Muslim mother, who for this reason was not Jewish, since the Jews reckon by the mother; a woman, whom Mehmet Effendi had described as a daughter of Jews; and a little boy, about whom I don't know what to say. Of one doubt I harbored I have already spoken. Now I will mention a second doubt: Obadiah had claimed to me, not once and not twice, that Mehmet Effendi had lied to Daniel when he told him that Luna was the daughter of Jews. Mehmet Effendi had wanted to please Daniel — had wanted to spare him suffering all his life — for had he known his wife was a Muslim, he would have felt guilty. Obadiah reiterated his claim that Luna was the daughter of Muslims. As for me, all I can do is present what I heard from one and what I heard from the other.

At that time, when we sat down at the Sabbath table in Daniel's house, all this was important. It was important for me to know, and I think that Daniel, too, gave it much thought. But now, after so many years, and after everything that happened, to whom does it matter?

11 The Boy's Tenth Birthday

After sundown, when everyone had left the orchard and there was not a living creature to be seen in the house or among the trees, I would go out to walk around the place until my legs were sore; and when I returned to the house, I had neither the strength nor the appetite to prepare myself a meal. After this I would lie down on my bed and read. Close to midnight I would get up and write in my diary, and if I was lucky I would then fall asleep for a few hours.

On those walks of mine in the orchard after sundown, when there was still some light in the sky, though among the trees there was an obscurity and a kind of fog, I again thought that I saw Luna appearing and disappearing as she always had. And again the thought occurred to me that it was the other Luna I was seeing. Once, she seemed to appear to me near the packing shed, and after a space of no time at all I was sure I saw her a long way off, next to the pool. It occasionally happened that I didn't restrain myself and called her by name, aloud. But she didn't look towards me, and this didn't surprise me. After all, she was deaf. And perhaps she wasn't even there at all.

One summer night, when I was lying in bed in a black mood, it seemed to me that I heard the bubbling of water from the direction of the pool. I got up and, without moving the shutter, peeped through the crack between its two halves. Did I really see a gleaming white body swimming in the pool? And after a while a woman came out of the pool and, instead of drying herself with a towel, stood on the edge of the railing, and the gentle night breeze made the beads of water fall from her. After that she went down the steps and vanished.

In 1935 Luna's son turned ten and a birthday party was held on a Sabbath, in the orchard house. A day earlier I asked him who had been invited. His answer was: First of all my Jewish father, and my Arab uncle and Mother and you, agronomist, of course you'll be with us. Apart from that there'll be people who are neither my grandfathers nor my grandmothers, neither uncles nor cousins.

I said: And who are they?

He replied: The head boatman and the customs officer and the deputy director of the Department of Agriculture and three fat growers and one thin one. And best of all I'm glad that Selim Baba is going to come, and we'll have fun.

Selim Baba was a Persian or perhaps an Arab. At any rate, he was the hero of Jaffa. He could carry three crates of fruit on his back all at once or lift heavy weights, bend iron horseshoes in his teeth, and tear a whole pack of cards between two fingers.

All of them actually did come on Saturday morning, some by car and some on foot, and immediately upon arriving they sat down in their armchairs on the veranda and started drinking arak and cognac, with nuts and pickled eggplant and confections for chasers, and soon they started singing aloud. But Luna and her son headed for the pool, and I saw them standing for a moment by the railing and laughing to each other, until the boy pushed his mother into the water and leaped right in after her. They swam in the water like two dolphins, diving and surfacing, chasing each other and spraying water with their mouths and hands.

I don't know how old Luna was when I first saw her, some twenty-two years before this, but I could see that the years had not left their mark on her. Twenty years after the day we are speaking of now, when her son was thirty, Luna looked younger than her son, and even younger than she had looked when I first saw her. On this occasion, on the boy's tenth birthday, I noticed this strange thing with absolute clarity, but I doubt if the others saw it.

While the mother and the son splashed around in the pool, and the guests enjoyed themselves on the veranda, Selim Baba appeared in the middle of the clearing below the pool. He spread out his legs and arms and puffed out his chest and announced that he was going to give us a display of his strength. All eyes turned towards the hero, and people on the veranda pulled their armchairs closer to the railing. Only Luna and her son did not interrupt their pranks in the water.

First of all, Selim Baba bound his chest with a chain and allowed the head boatman to examine its links and to tie it tightly around his body, and then he started beathing in and expanding his lungs until he cracked the chain and it fell to the earth, its links clanging against each other loudly in the surrounding silence. A roar of cheering and clapping rose from the veranda. Then he took an iron rod that had heavy stones attached to both ends and raised it above his head with one swing. Again he received a loud ovation. Finally, he proclaimed in a loud voice and with grandiloquent phrases that he was willing to wrestle three men, whoever they might be. But not one person there accepted the invitation.

Then the director of the Department of Agriculture, a drunken and foolish Gentile who was nevertheless cunning and a practical joker, suggested a stupid thing: he said that all the men there should form pairs to wrestle with each other. The winners out of each pair would all go and wrestle with Selim Baba, all of them together. Selim Baba accepted the proposal and the Gentile called loudly: Who's first?

Then Daniel got up — Daniel the gentle, the quiet and refined, a man who wouldn't touch a fly on the wall — and said: I will wrestle with my brother, Obadiah.

The two of them climbed down from the veranda, in their festive attire, and took up positions in the middle of the clearing beneath the pool, while Selim Baba made room for them. They stood facing each other like two cocks, eyes fixed on each other, awaiting the signal.

Go! cried the Gentile.

At the very moment the two of them leaped at each other, I saw Luna and her son interrupt their game and come to the edge of the pool to grip the railing and raise their heads out of the water to watch the spectacle.

When the Gentile called "Go," I saw what Obadiah did, and I was astounded: he jumped at his opponent, grabbed the inside part of the tie Daniel was wearing around his neck, and pulled it with all his might. That idea couldn't have come to him just then, on the spur of the moment. I believe that Obadiah had meditated on this occasion for many days and years before this, or perhaps he was used to it from other fights and wrestling matches about which I knew nothing. At any rate it looked as if he would finish Daniel off, strangling him to death on the spot. But Daniel, whose neck muscles were strong — stronger, it appeared, than one would have guessed by appearances — pulled himself backwards a step or two, swung up his right leg, and kicked Obadiah in the chest, knocking him to the ground. Before Obadiah had time to recover and get up, Daniel tore the tie from around his neck and threw it away. Now the two brothers were tightly locked together, each trying to raise the other up in the air and throw him heavily back down onto the ground. They resembled two men in a primitive dance, wild and savage, a dance in appearance only, but in truth the last embrace before death.

The people on the veranda immediately divided into two camps. The head boatman and the customs manager called cries of encouragement to Obadiah, while the Jewish growers supported Daniel. The deputy director of the Department of Agriculture appointed himself referee and stood looking on with a frozen face. And Luna's son and his mother looked on in silence from the pool.

One moment the brothers were locked together, and the next they tore apart from each other; and when they did that, each of them was left with scraps of the other's shirt or clothing in his hand, so that after several minutes they no longer looked like two reputable growers but resembled a pair of robbers who had met in a dark alley and fallen upon each other for plunder. Very soon they showed scratches and wounds, with blood streaming from their noses and sweat pouring from their foreheads, their dishevelled hair covering their eyes; all you could hear was their breathing, the sound of a bellows with its skin burst.

Now the two appeared weary and their movements grew slow and heavy, and on the veranda everyone was quiet. Each would now retreat a little, to get some air, and then they would approach each other again, land blows upon each other, almost according to some predetermined order, or as if taking turns. Their strength was clearly running out, and in fact after a while they both fell down and lay on the ground with their arms and legs spread out. Then I gathered courage and ran to where Daniel had fallen, to see if he was still alive. And the Gentile on the veranda went down to examine Obadiah. They were both breathing heavily, with their eyes closed. I hurried to Daniel's car and drove to the English doctor, the same doctor I had called for Mehmet Effendi at the time.

Thus ended the boy's tenth birthday.

A year later, in 1936, the blood riots burst out again in the land of Israel, and again Arabs slaughtered Jews. But this time we were ready.

12 From the Moskobiyeh to Jericho

All in all, I understood why Daniel had gone down there to wrestle with his brother. Even before it happened, I should have realized that under the veneer of total reconciliation there pulsed in Daniel a repressed hatred as deep as his love for Luna. But as to why Obadiah hated Daniel — so much as to actually fall upon him with such murderous fury, to really try to kill him —that was hard for me to understand. Did he hate his brother because their father had abandoned his mother, so many years ago, weeping and lost in Constantinople? Yet this father, and Daniel's mother, too, had treated Obadiah with love and respect and had done whatever he wanted, even though he had been a source of constant trouble to them. And as for Daniel's treatment of his brother — were greater decency and fairness conceivable? Was Obadiah incapable of comparing his miserable situation with Mehmet Effendi, when he slept on a mat in the packing shed, to his situation in Daniel's house, first in the special modern room he had had built for him, and afterwards in his splendid home in Tel Aviv? Did he think that Daniel also had an obligation to put the property in Obadiah's name? And the fact that Daniel let him share his wife's sheets — wasn't that enough? Wasn't it too much? Much more than one could even conceive?

Well, it appeared that Obadiah had not forgiven his brother for the fact that he, too — Daniel, the husband and provider —had come to Luna and loved her with a love more desperate and more terrible than any. For if it wasn't Daniel's love of Luna, what else could have caused Obadiah to desire the death of his brother, the son of his own father?

A man like me, who has nothing in his world other than earth and trees, may possibly be incapable of understanding the power of a man's love for a woman. But when I think of Daniel — whose love for the orchard did not fall much below his love for Luna, and, if one may say so, they were one to him — then I imagine it might be possible for a man to lose his mind because of a woman, too; and in the final analysis it is possible that Daniel and I are not as different from each other as would appear at first glance.

And where did Luna's son stand on all this? This is a question I put to myself a long time ago, and over the years I received a clear answer.

On his bar mitzvah, Luna's son got a pistol as a present from his father. That was what he had wanted, and Daniel fulfilled the boy's request with a heavy heart, giving him stern warnings. Afterwards, when he started showing the boy how to take care of the weapon, how to strip it down and reassemble it, he was startled to find that the boy was no less versed in it than he was. He did not know — and I didn't tell him — that at the orchard house, under the stone settee along the wall of the parlor, Luna's son had his own store of weapons, collected over a long period of time, which he was careful to keep well-oiled and wrapped in strips of cloth, according to all the rules for storing weapons of this kind.

Occasionally I would feel guilty about having become a partner to Luna's son in keeping his secret from Daniel. But I wanted to maintain relations of trust with the boy. Were I to lose his trust, I would have been left more alone than a man can bear to be.

Luna's son would come to the orchard house almost every day after school. He also lived with me in the orchard during summer vacations and all the festival vacations.

During the summer, between irrigations, I would put one of the veteran workers in charge of the work he was expert in, and Luna's son and I would set out to tour the countryside. At first we visited places near Jaffa. I brought him to the Moskobiyeh, the Russian church near Tabitha's grave, so he could see Selim Ayub's orchard, where the Shamuti strain was first discovered. And on that occasion I told him that the very first Jewish pioneers who had come to revivify the wilderness of our country — the Bilu people — had lived in Selim Ayub's orchard, which shows that not all the Arabs had been against us and that there had been days of co-operation. But Luna's son shrugged his shoulders: And what did the boatmen in Jaffa do? Doesn't most of their income come from the Jews, from the oranges we send and the money they earn by carrying Jewish passengers from the ships? And still they slaughtered thirty new immigrants at the Immigrant Center in the port. Don't talk rubbish, agronomist. That was how he concluded, without affectation, but from the depths of his heart. And I wasn't angry at him.

From the Moskobiyeh we went to Mikveh-Israel, so that he could see the botanical gardens and the underground wine press and the boys studying agriculture. He didn't want to enter into conversation with the boys, perhaps out of shyness, but in the botanical gardens he asked me about every single plant, and after we had gone some distance and were wandering over the rocky ground between the agricultural college and Tel-Er-Rish, he kept bending down to the ground to pick a small weed or a tiny flower or a handful of dried stamens, raising them up to my nose and asking me to smell them. And for every weed or flower he asked me: Agronomist, do you know what this is? And I admitted that I didn't know, and he would then tell me the name of every one of them, and I was astonished and asked him where he had acquired all this knowledge.

From my mother, he replied.

How come? I said. Do you go walking in the fields with your mother?

Sure, all the time, said Luna's son. And he leaped up into the air like a wild colt, then landed flat on the ground and, with one hand stretched out before him, caught a kind of grasshopper that generally passes unseen because it is earth-colored and no larger than a bee. And about this grasshopper he also had wonderful tales to tell me, until I was dazed.

When do you go walking with your mother? I interrogated him again.

I told you, all the time.

In the orchard, too? I didn't give up questioning.

Why not? In the orchard, too.

And your father? I had said something silly.

Father? Luna's son repeated my question. Father knows how to do accounts in a notebook and how to read books and travel abroad.

Your father's a very clever man, I said firmly.

Of course he's clever, said the boy. All the Jews are clever.

All the Jews? And aren't you a Jew?

Sure, I'm a Jew. I think so, he said, laughing.

I didn't know how to continue the conversation, so I walked behind him, listening to the names he called out for the plants, some of them in Arabic and some in Hebrew, and when we found a plant whose Latin name I knew, I would tell him, so that he might see I wasn't just a reed-cutter. He would repeat the name aloud, as if testing it on his tongue. Generally the Latin names didn't appeal to him, and he would mutilate them, pronouncing them as if they were Arabic names. When I showed him *Solanum Nigrum,* he said: What? *Sulam* (which in Hebrew means "ladder"), what kind of *sulam*? And when I named the only pine that stood on the nearby hill, and told him it was called *"Pinus amigdalus,"* the boy said: That sounds right. It really looks like a little *migdal,* which in Hebrew means "tower."

And on other walks we got as far as Ramle and Lydda, and together we climbed to the top of the tower of the White Fathers, where bats flew around and fled from us. We also went down to the underground pools and finally dined in the house of one of the Arabs of Lydda, an acquaintance of mine, where that day they were pouring gold bars into thick heavy clay containers, and the boy asked me what the Arab sheikh was going to do with this gold and where he had got it. I told him of the herds of camels this Arab possessed, and about the smuggling and the hashish trade in the caravans traveling from Lebanon to Egypt, through the deserts of the Sinai. Luna's son listened with great interest, but when he heard that all this gold would be hidden underground, for years and for generations, he laughed and said the Arab was an utter fool.

And with the passage of time we started making our trips by bus, and I took him to Jericho and Bethlehem and Jerusalem, and when he got a bit bigger, able to use his fists when necessary, I wasn't afraid of even taking him to Gaza, which was notorious as a city of toughs who did grievous injury to any stranger or foreigner, with no apparent excuse or reason.

When Luna's son was about fifteen or sixteen, he started going off on his trips alone and I didn't always know where he was going, but I was confident of his safe return. Mostly he would come back with stones, rock fragments, plants, and insects in his knapsack. It also happened that he would return without shoes or knapsack, scratched and dusty but in high spirits, and would respond to my questions with a smile and silence. And if I pushed him he would say: Agronomist, you're terribly inquisitive. And I would be obliged to be content with his scolding and to smile with him.

13 Another War

The world war broke out in 1939, but we did not feel its impact until the beginning of 1941. During the months after Passover, Italian planes bombed Tel Aviv. But that wasn't our only trouble. We were facing a difficult crisis, with no chance of exporting our fruit, while the orchard continued making its own demands: fertilizers and manure, water and expensive workdays for which the workers had to be paid, even if you didn't need the fruit. True, the government had bought some oranges for the army in Palestine and neighboring countries, but that was not enough to cover the losses. Nor can it be said that the Department of Agriculture ignored the growers' difficulties. It gave small subsidies and a few loans at low interest rates. It was heartbreaking to see what was happening in the orchards, especially in those neglected by their owners. A kind of abandon spread through the world, and at night soldiers strolled through the city streets — Australians and New Zealanders and Englishmen and South Africans, Americans and Negroes and Indians —all of them drunk, their pockets full of money, assaulting girls and women and smashing shop windows, while the shopkeepers remained silent, because during the day they earned their living from these soldiers, and they were better off remaining silent. But oder was completely disrupted.

I myself didn't feel all these things I have listed, because I spent all my time in the orchard, until the rioting reached my own threshold. One night I heard voices under my window, and I went out to look. There was a gang of Arabs, snatching up tools and fruit and loading them on their donkeys.

Who's there? I called out in a loud voice, from where I stood on the steps.

Shut up, Jew, an arrogant voice answered me. Go to sleep.

Your mother's cunt, I said to him. Get your bones away from here, you and all you whoresons.

They understood no other language, and I had to show firmness and speak in obscenities if I wanted to stay alive.

Except this time I wasn't so successful. Among the gang was

someone with a gun, and suddenly I heard a shot and felt a sharp blow to my shoulder. Had I wanted to, I could have stayed on my feet, but a sudden thought told me it would be better to fall to the ground. If they thought they'd killed me, perhaps they might flee for their lives. But if they saw I was only wounded, they would come up the steps to finish me off.

And I was right. The cowardly sons-of-Belial urged on their donkeys and fled. Then I grabbed my shoulder and started feeling pain and touching blood. I was alone until morning, when some people came to the orchard and took me to a hospital in Tel Aviv.

And who came to visit me in the hospital? Of course, Daniel came. And even Obadiah. And had Luna's son been in town, he would undoubtedly have come. But he was already over sixteen and had gone to one of the kibbutzim to serve in one of our underground regiments, the ones that later were called the Palmach and had been set up to fight the Germans if they invaded from the direction of the Western Desert, and that finally fought — after the end of the world war — the English and the Arabs. But all this doesn't belong to my subject. Whoever will write the story of orchardry in Palestine will also write about the Palmach.

But who else came to visit me in the hospital? Well, Luna came. It was unbelievable! And not only did she come, but on that very occasion she made clear signs to Daniel that he should give instructions to have me taken out of the hospital and moved to their home. She was very firm about this, and three days later the doctors allowed me to be carried to Daniel's house, where I spent three weeks until I recovered. To me those three weeks were like a dream, like something unimaginable. Luna did not let any one else — neither doctor nor nurse — look after me; she herself washed me and fed me and changed my bandages and shaved my beard, since I was unable to move my arm because of the bandage. Not only that, but she sat by my side for hours on end, like one who comes to entertain a patient with pleasant discourse so as to distract him from his pains. Of course, she did not speak a word to me. After all, she is a mute.

And then I got this crazy idea and said to myself: What can happen if I speak to her and ask her a few questions? If she hears me, perhaps she'll answer me; and if she doesn't hear, then certainly no reason why I shouldn't speak. So I said: Luna, what do you do in the orchard in the twilight hours? And how do you appear in different places at one and the same time? And is it true that you spoke with Obadiah, in his room beside the packing shed, when you were alone with him? And why was your face frozen, as always, when Obadiah tried to kill Daniel at your son's birthday party? And when do you go walking in the fields with the boy and teach him the names of plants and insects?

I looked at her as I spoke, and saw that her face was sealed. But that face was not lacking in feeling during the days she sat by my bed. I am not exaggerating when I say it expressed agony or dread. Yet the slightest shadow of friendship, like some distant affection, was stamped in her face, and I didn't know how or why I had earned this from her. For many years I thought deeply about the reasons for her devotion to me during my convalescence, and in the course of time I wove together a certain idea, and perhaps there is some truth in it. Perhaps in Luna's eyes I was the last man who connected her to the memories of her youth. Whether she was a child of a Jew or a Muslim, for her I was both; for I was of the first settlers and spoke the language of the Arabs like one of them. With the passage of time my face had grown tanned and my skin sunburned, and I looked like one of the Arab fellaheen, who are perhaps the surviving traces of those primitive Jews who never went into exile and gradually became assimilated with the country's Muslim inhabitants. Perhaps Luna thought that I was the ancient link connecting Obadiah's race to Daniel's; for if truth be told, she, in her deafness and dumbness, faithfully served both together, sharing her favors between them — if not equally, then according to the degree of the demands and firmness of each, according to their changing temperaments during the changing days.

I doubt if another explanation can be found for that passing devotion I received from Luna, after having fallen victim to the ancient feud between her two husbands.

Finally I recovered my health and returned to the orchard house and lived there until the war ended. And after that, too. And I would still be living there to this day, had it not been for what happened.

14 Luna's Son Refuses to Study Agriculture

About a year and a half after these things, the English armies struck at the German invaders in the Western Desert, and we breathed more freely. During those days reliable information reached us about what the Germans were doing to the Jews in Europe. We did not know then if tens of thousands or millions of Jews were involved, but it was clear to us what degree of debasement the detested Germans had reached. Thus, when the English attacked the abomination of the human race in the Western Desert, and the whole world already knew what the Germans had done to us, we believed that the English government would permit refugees from the Holocaust to reach safely the shores of the land of Israel. At the time there were several ships at sea laden with Jews — mostly ramshackle and decaying ships our people had bought from their owners, paying their captains the fares for the journey. Now it turned out that not only did the English government refuse to permit these Jews to reach us, but their troops were firing at these ships while still on the open sea, sinking them with all their passengers. And if a skillful captain did not manage to reach secretly, under the dark cover of night, the shores of our country, the English soldiers would capture the people on board and imprison them in concentration camps in Cyprus and Mauritius.

And then, when Daniel said to Luna's son: The Germans have been beaten in the desert, and it's time for you to leave the Palmach and return home and start going to agricultural college at Kfar Tabor, the boy laughed and said: What we learned to do to the Germans we'll now do to the English. And if the Arabs join our enemies, we'll teach them a few tricks in hand-to-hand combat.

These hand-to-hand combat exercises were actually only stick fights. In the Palmach they were teaching them to fight hand-to-hand with sticks.

And instead of going to study at the agricultural college, Luna's son remained with his fellows in the kibbutzim.

When the war ended, in 1945, it was possible to hope that

life would return to normal and that we would return to the orchard, to bring it back to life and be nourished by its fruits; but history thought otherwise. Not one day passed without mines exploding on the roads, not one week passed without people killed — Jews, Englishmen, Arabs.

The Jews demanded free immigration to the land of Israel for the remaining survivors of the slaughter; the Arabs opposed this, and the English did the Arabs' will, because they sensed that if the Jewish population in the land of Israel increased, in the end they would establish an independent state, and that would be the end of the English conquest of Palestine — the very conquest we had greeted with cheers and processions and dancing in 1918. Now the English and the Arabs joined forces against us, and each of our underground organizations fought against our enemies in its own way and according to its own understanding.

And they even fought among themselves. Only Luna's son did not discriminate between one organization and another, and wherever killing or mine-laying or an explosion occurred, he would go there and volunteer to participate in the work. Just as his mother would appear in different parts of the orchard at one and the same time, one day he would blow up bridges in Achziv with the Palmach people, the next day he would be shooting with the Irgun Tzvai Leumi at the High Commissioner's car at the entrance to Jerusalem, and a day later he would kill the head of the secret police. I don't have hard information about this — I am relating it only from hearsay. But it's reasonable to believe that the apple doesn't fall far from the tree, and if Luna was like that, then her son was all the more so.

All that time I lived in the orchard, trying to preserve it to the best of my ability, and Daniel bore the burden with me, as was his way. Just the two of us. Obadiah was busy, running between Tel Aviv and Jaffa, between Jaffa and Ramle, between Ramle and Jerusalem. We didn't ask him what he was doing. Even if we had asked he wouldn't have answered. Until one day, when Luna's son came home to rest for one night in his bed and take a real bath in the bathtub, he said to Daniel: Tell my Arab uncle that if he wants to stay alive, he had better stop wandering around the country. His actions are known, and if he doesn't stop, I'll see to it that he stops all actions, in general and in particular.

He had a new style of talking now, one I had not heard before. Daniel, too, was surprised and said to him that an uncle is always an uncle and that the trade of killing should not be brought into the family. In the family, said Daniel, all quarrels are verbal and in the end are settled in peace and understanding.

Anyone who talks of peace today will lie in peace on his bed, said Luna's son, speaking poetry, a kind of common popular saying. And whoever wants life had better not talk of peace. After the war there'll be peace. And in wartime it isn't lips that speak, but rifle barrels.

As much as all that? said Daniel, mockingly.

As much as all that, my Jewish father, the youth replied meaningfully. And I do not know if Daniel got the full import of what he meant.

At all events, he did not kill his uncle, even though his uncle Obadiah did not desist from his good deeds. On the contrary: when the riots increased in the country, from the beginning of 1947 until the day of the partition of Palestine into two states —a Jewish one and an Arab one — Obadiah intensified his activities and used his former room, the one next to the packing shed, as a kind of meeting place for his friends. At night from my veranda above the pool, I could see them coming from all sides of the orchard, through holes they had made in the fence and in the main gate, and gathering in the room which Daniel had built for Obadiah.

Once Obadiah gave me a hint, saying he wondered why I didn't fear for my life; why I didn't go to Tel Aviv until the furor died down. And when I didn't take the hint, he uttered a kind of warning, saying he couldn't take on himself the responsibility for my safety.

I'll worry about my own safety, I said to him. And you, you should pray to God, so that I needn't worry about yours as well. You'd better find other worriers.

That was how I answered him in the summer of 1947, and from then on we did not exchange another word until the day when Obadiah tried to kill me, on the thirteenth of May in 1948. On that day we exchanged a few more words, for the last time.

15 The Orchard Is Captured Anew, This Being the Beginning of Its End

When I saw how far things had gone, I acted deviously and cunningly. Above the parlor of the orchard house there was an attic with a wooden floor, the floor being the ceiling of the parlor. I secretly started storing provisions there — canned food and jugs of water, as well as a rifle and a pistol and a supply of ammunition. Then I cut a thin crack in the attic floor, which I could peep through into the parlor. When this work was done, I informed the orchard workers that I was going to live in Tel Aviv until peace came. That night I went up into the attic, and with Daniel's consent I spent about half a year there, until our armies entered Jaffa on the thirteenth of May in 1948.

During the day I would sleep in the attic, with the cocked rifle beside my bed. And in the evening I would get up and relieve myself into a bucket, which I would empty later on, after midnight, into a pit among the trees. From the day I announced I was leaving the orchard, Obadiah had come and taken over the house for himself and his gang. They would sit in the parlor and talk, making decisions and distributing weapons to young rowdies, who now came to the place openly, saluting Obadiah as if he were a high-ranking officer, and listening to his orders.

At regular intervals Luna's son would come to the orchard in the early hours of the morning. During the night he would skirt the patrols between Tel Aviv and Jaffa and walk through alleys he knew from childhood, to appear suddenly in my attic, listen to what I had heard and seen in the parlor, and return to Tel Aviv that same night. Occasionally he brought me fresh food, fruits and vegetables, or a cooked dish from the kitchen, refreshing my spirits.

One night no one remained in the parlor save Obadiah and an Arab, Salame by name, who was commander of the gangs in the Ramle region. They were drinking arak and bragging garrulously. In those days the Arabs had a pleasant and spicy subject for conversation: they would expatiate on the day when they would conquer Tel Aviv.

That night, when Obadiah and Salame were alone, they discussed the same subject, when suddenly Salame asked Obadiah: And what are you going to do with Daniel?

What I should have done the day he arrived here, and didn't do. Cursed be the man who drove the first nail into the ship that brought him here! said Obadiah.

You good-for-nothing, I said to myself as I sat above their heads in the attic, my hands trembling with fury and wanting to grab the rifle and smash his skull. You good-for-nothing; is this how you repay all the good that Daniel has done you?

Bravo, Salame said to him. I was afraid you'd turn coward and not know your duty on the day of victory.

You'll see, Obadiah boasted, and the two of them clinked their glasses together.

Several nights later, Luna's son came and I told him what I had heard.

Meanwhile the days of decision approached, but I did not see with my own eyes what happened in Jaffa during the last days before the conquest. Several weeks later I heard from one of the growers — a friend of Daniel's, Yitzhak Rokeach by name — what he had heard from Mina Tanos, a customs officer of Jaffa port. And this is what Yitzhak Rokeach told me: I asked Mina Tanos what happened in Jaffa port during the last days, after the conquest of Jaffa by the Jews, and this was his answer:

Some twenty days before the surrender of Jaffa to the Jewish army, the Arabs felt the end was drawing near. Anyone who could find means of transport packed a few belongings and fled with his family to one of the Arab cities. The poor, who had no means with which to hire transport and were unable to flee to the Arab cities, locked their houses and went down to the quay, hoping to sail on one of the ships, which, according to rumors that had been spread among them, Egypt was sending for the purpose. Some 25,000 people — men, women, and children —thronged the quay and occupied the warehouses and offices they had broken into.

The boatmen first took their own families in the large barges, two or three of which were attached to a tugboat. Some of them sailed for Gaza, some for Port Said, and some for Tyre, Sidon, or

Beirut. A few of these returned to Jaffa and loaded more men, women, and children onto their boats, in difficult conditions and at exorbitant prices. These trips were dangerous, and there were even rumors that there had been several drownings. Two steamships — one Swedish and one Egyptian, both of them freighters — took hundreds of refugees on board, and in comparison to the conditions on the Arab boats the journey in these ships was comfortable. On the quay some seven hundred people remained. There were still some forty or fifty barges in port, some in serviceable condition, but not one tugboat was left to tow them. So they stayed.

Meanwhile the Iraqi and Jordanian soldiers spread out from the town to the port and started plundering and looting, as they had done earlier in the city itself. The soldiers broke into the warehouses and started selling all the merchandise they found there at any price, on condition they were paid in gold or silver. The Arab "Rescue Committee," headed by Abu Laban, tried to stop the looting, but in vain, and the situation grew more critical by the hour. The soldiers did not content themselves with looting but also raped women and girls.

And what did the officers do? asked Yitzhak Rokeach.

Mina Tanos nodded his head and replied: The officers? They participated with the soldiers in their rioting!

What I heard with my own ears, and what I saw during those days, has to do only with Obadiah and his circle of friends. One night, in the parlor of the orchard house, a conversation occurred about the departure from Jaffa. I understood that the Jews were allowing any Arab who so wished to take his property, load it on a truck or a cart, and leave Jaffa.

And the Jews don't shoot at those who leave? asked one of the Arabs.

They don't shoot, his friend confirmed. They stand at the entry to Mikveh-Israel, with weapons in their hands, look at the cars, and don't do a thing.

And what do you think, Abdullah? some of them said.

I'm staying, said Abdullah.

The Jews will kill you, they said to him.

The Jews won't do a thing to me, he replied confidently. I know them.

As you wish, his friends said. We're leaving.

And on the thirteenth of May in 1948, the members of the Arab "Rescue Committee" of Jaffa came out, with Abu Laban at their head and waving white flags, and handed the city over to the Jews.

When, from my attic, I heard voices speaking Hebrew in the orchard, I climbed down the ladder. From the corridor I passed through the parlor. Obadiah sat there in an armchair, smoking a cigarette and looking straight ahead. He didn't see me pass. Outside, beside the pool, I found several of our fellows, with weapons in their hands. They were surprised to see me. I asked them to contact Tel Aviv and inform Daniel that I was whole and healthy.

Less than two hours later Luna's son appeared in the yard.

Where is he? he asked.

Upstairs in the big room, I told him.

He beckoned me to follow him, and the two of us climbed the stairs and went into the dining hall. Obadiah rose to greet us, smiling and offering us his hand.

Where were you these last months, Uncle? said Luna's son, without smiling or putting out his hand.

In the orchard, of course, said Obadiah very calmly. Who do you think looked after the orchard all this time, if not me? The agronomist ran off. . . . And he looked at me with contemptuous pity.

The agronomist didn't run off, said Luna's son.

He ran off. And how he ran off! He took off for Tel Aviv even before the first shot was fired, said Obadiah. Had I not been here, they would have burned the house down and pulled up all the trees.

The agronomist didn't run off, Luna's son repeated.

What is this, a joke? Obadiah cried out in anger. You want to make fun of me?

Start walking, Luna's son ordered him. March.

Where to? asked Obadiah in wonder.

Out into the hall.

At the dark end of the corridor, behind a heap of discarded furniture, Luna's son showed him the ladder leaning there against the wall. Climb, he told him. We'll come up after you.

Where to? Now Obadiah's voice was high and slightly hoarse.

Up. Straight up.

He climbed like someone who'd seen a ghost, with us behind him, and the three of us entered the attic, which was as it had been all that time — dark, with a bed in the middle, and food scattered all around, and on the bed a rifle and a pistol.

Obadiah tried to pretend surprise, as if we had brought him here to show him the marvels of this house before he deigned to buy it from us. Then Luna's son pushed him in the shoulder and said to him:

Bend down to the floor. Bend down!

Obadiah bent down in fright, and then Luna's son pushed him downwards by the nape of his neck, until his nose hit the crack I had made in the floor.

Tell us what you see, my Arab uncle, said Luna's son. Or would you prefer the agronomist to tell us what he has seen here in the last few months?

Obadiah got up from where he lay, shook the dust from his trousers, looked at us with a numbed face, and said: It's all a lie. It's all a total lie.

What's a lie? Luna's son pressed him. Who's a lie?

Obadiah took several steps into the middle of the attic, leaped towards the bed, and snatched up the pistol. Luna's son kicked him and the pistol fell to the floor. I picked it up and also grabbed hold of the rifle.

Don't shoot him, Luna's son said to me.

I didn't intend to shoot him, I said.

Climb down, he said to Obadiah.

When we got to the parlor, Luna's son ordered me to take two hoes, the ones we used to hoe the garden, and to remove the handles from them. When I had done so, he took one stick in his hand and offered the other to Obadiah and said: We're going down to the yard, and there we'll hold a contest; and just as you fought with my father, now you'll fight with me.

Obadiah had no choice. He understood what faced him.

Our fellows who had been here before had left, and now the orchard was empty, it seemed. Only the three of us stood in the yard, beneath the pool.

Selim Baba! Luna's son yelled into the air. Give the signal, we're ready.

Then he turned to me and said: Go back to the veranda and watch from there, and applaud the victor. Go on, agronomist, get up there and enjoy yourself.

When I had done as he had told me, I saw from the distance how he made a sign with his eyes to his uncle, and how they took positions for battle.

A stick-fight is no exhilarating sight, and I don't have the heart to tell what I saw there. We carried Obadiah's body together, and together we dug him a grave by the orchard fence, where we hid his body.

We had turned toward the orchard house and were already a long way away from the fence, when I felt a sudden urge to look back. My old madness had risen inside my brain.

Luna stood there, over the grave, her hands folded on her lap and her face serene as usual. She gazed straight ahead, at the row of trees opposite.

16 Daniel and I Betray Our Mission

Most of that year, battles were going on everywhere. The armies of seven Arab states invaded us and the country was like a cauldron. Only in Jaffa was it quiet, and I went out into the stricken city to see who of my acquaintances had remained there. All the growers, the big merchants, and financiers had fled. Only the poorest of the poor remained, and these sheep who had lost their shepherds gathered together inside a few streets, south of the port, along the waterfront. What would happen to the orchards that had been abandoned, and to the commerce that had stopped? And how would these miserable souls support themselves, now that their leaders had abandoned them?

I went out into the wasted city and was immediately surrounded by some dozens of Arabs, who fell upon me with pleading and cajoling. One wanted to know where his boatman son was; if he had been arrested, perhaps I could ask about him, perhaps they would allow his mother to take him some bread and cheese at the jail; another asked about his aged wife, who had fallen sick, and there was no one to find her a doctor since Jaffa's Arab doctors had fled together with the rest of the notables.

I tried to fulfill all their requests to the best of my ability. I went to our military governors and found acquaintances there and pestered them with requests, and generally I was successful. Especially as there was nothing urgent to be done in the orchard at this time. The current season had been completely spoiled, and again the fruit would go to waste. So I traipsed from one office to another, to save at least those few who saw me as their saviour.

I had lived all my life with these people, I had seen them in the days of their strength and their courage, and now the immensity of their fall was heartbreaking.

My neglect of the orchard during that period was indeed criminal, even though, as I have said, there was nothing urgent to be done in the orchard at that time, and even had I stayed there from morning till night, I doubt if I would have been of any use to anyone, and certainly I myself would have felt a terrible desolation. A kind of emptying-out was occurring there, around the house and among the trees. And is it an easy thing to see the entire population of a big city suddenly evaporate into air, overnight?

But Daniel's collapse was greater than mine.

At first I thought he was keeping away from the orchard because he had financial matters to put in order and commercial worries; for in the orchard itself there was nothing urgent that needed doing in that crazy year. The routine jobs did not need my presence more than once every ten days, and Daniel's presence wasn't needed at all. For this reason I didn't give any thought to the strange fact that I hadn't seen Daniel for two whole weeks. Until one night, when I was in my room in the orchard house, I heard a knock on my door and called, Come in. Daniel entered, and the way he entered was just like the way he had appeared during those nights that were not his own, during those many nights since his marriage to Luna.

I greeted him and drew up an armchair for him, and then went to the kitchen to put a kettle on. When I came back, I found him in absolute dejection. He was pale, his head hung down to his chest, and his breathing was heavy.

Are you sick? I asked him. What's the matter, Daniel?

Daniel raised his head and smiled miserably. He said to me: I'm not sick. But maybe I'm already dead.

I said: Couldn't you find a better joke than that to tell me?

Daniel didn't answer and remained silent until the water in the kettle boiled. I went out to make tea, and when I came back, he was still silent. I saw I would have to act firmly if I wanted to get to the bottom of his secret and try to help him.

Why did you leave Luna at home alone? The son's in the army, and she's alone.

I have nothing to say to Luna, he replied.

What do you have to say to her? I jested. Play cards with her. Go to the cinema. Are there so few things a man can do with his wife?

My friend, said Daniel, and he looked at me as if from a great distance. If we had to kill Obadiah to prove how right we are, perhaps we are not so right after all?

Does Luna blame you for Obadiah's death? I asked.

Luna doesn't blame. She accepts any judgment, any event. If I had to look to her response to know if I had acted rightly or not, I would never know. She leaves me to examine my actions according to my understanding.

And what have you discovered in your understanding? I was curt with him, for anger was growing in me.

I concluded that if we killed Obadiah, it means we couldn't face the truth he bore in his soul while he still lived.

Idle philosophizing! I threw in his face. All your life you've wanted to be more righteous than the Creator demands of his creatures. You make me angry! Daniel, shake yourself out of this stupor, take hold of your wife and rejoice in her. She's yours now, all yours, as she never was before.

She was much more mine when I dreamed her on board the ship, Daniel said softly. Then, then she was all mine. Even though during those days she was only Obadiah's, in the lower world.

A woman is not a thing for the higher worlds, I called out in a voice louder than I had intended. Women in Paradise is a Muslim belief. Hold her, Daniel, I urge you — hold her fast. See how beautiful she is, she's young as a girl. She doesn't look a year older than when I first saw her nearly thirty years ago.

Daniel must have thought I was speaking metaphorically, trying to praise Luna. But I really meant it, this marvelous thing I have already mentioned: Luna had not aged even one day. At the very most, one could say that now she was the same age as her son.

And because Daniel kept silent, I seized the opportunity to strike while the iron was still hot, and said: What are you waiting for? For someone else to come and take her from you again? Hold her, man. Do you hear or don't you?

Now I am again not sure if she is mine, said Daniel quietly, as is he were quoting some verdict pronounced in another world.

You're her husband, you're the man who loves her more than any other man does. Obadiah's dead. If you go on talking like this, your manhood, too, will be taken from you.

It may have already been taken, said Daniel. I'm afraid to

touch her. Perhaps I also don't want to touch her.

That night I didn't understand what he was talking about. But he came to visit me again, at the orchard house, and stayed with me all night, as in the days I thought had passed, never to return. But they did return, in their entirety. Daniel feared Luna. Whether he was awed by the great happiness now within his reach, or whether something else frightened him, something more terrible than a dream fulfilled — that I do not know. But I knew this was no passing madness, but an essence branded in his soul. Just as a seaman does not know how to walk confidently on shore, just as the prisoner, released from jail, cannot stand the light of the sun, and just as the hen does not know how to fly because for thousands of years it has lived in a coop, so in Daniel's blood there was some heritage that paralyzed him at the very moment a broad space for movement opened up before him, and his limbs were unable to move.

My brother, I said to him, I would rather be dead than see you like this.

It may be that we're both already dead, said Daniel. It may be that we're speaking from out of the dream on the other side of life.

Yet at the time we were people who had just reconquered their land in storm and blood.

Except it seems we were wrought from inferior material: when we were liberated from the enemy's death-embrace, and he lay dead at our feet, we thought that embraces of love were gone from the world, and that the dead were our own flesh and blood.

17 Luna's Son Decorates His Mother

On a Sabbath Eve I was invited to Daniel's house, after not having dined at their table for more than half a year. This time there were four of us, not five. The son had received leave from the army and had come to spend the Sabbath at home, and when the time came to sit down at the table, Luna lit the candles, and this time — the wonder of it! — she took a prayer book in her hands and looked at what was written there and moved her lips without making a sound. She had never before made the blessing over the candles, only lighting them as Daniel had commanded her.

I observed her during the meal, to see if I might discover what it was that had put dread in Daniel's heart, and I found no sign of displeasure or anger in her: she was serene, beautiful as on the day I first met her, when she had stood beside us to serve us with pleasant movements and light in her face that held no shadow or the shadow of a shadow.

That evening my mind was set on investigations, and I took special note of the dishes she had prepared for us. For the first time since eating at their table, I observed something I had not noticed previously: the type of food and the spices used were a mixture of Jewish cooking, such as we had known in our parents' homes, with Arab cooking, such as I had grown accustomed to since I first tasted an Arab dish more than forty years ago. So, I said to myself, Obadiah's still sitting at the table with us, in some kind of indirect and symbolic way. And when I looked at the people eating, I saw that they were all quite pleased with the dishes and, it seemed to me, they would not have wanted to exchange them for others. And if that was indeed so, it could be that Daniel's madness was not madness at all, and he had sensed and felt something that I, too, ought to know thoroughly.

Several more months passed, and just as all things in the world have their hour, until it passes to be replaced by another hour, more beautiful or more difficult, so also the war came to an end, and the amazement that had overcome Daniel was also replaced by an apparent calm and equilibrium, and Luna's son returned from the army and went to study at the Haifa Technion, and all that he had missed during the emergency period he made up in half the time in peacetime, and if I say of him that he was quick of mind and very talented, I still haven't said a thing.

Daniel and I returned to our orchard work, as if it was the most natural thing to do, and it seemed that only pleasures and large profits and the joy of doing awaited us there; but the truth was that something had been damaged, perhaps irreparably. Not the orchard, God forbid. The spirit was not what it had been at the beginning. If in previous days we had worked hard — but with joy — to win out over the stupidity of customs people, the corruption of policemen, and the laziness of officials, while convinced that on the day we got rid of them all we would experience triumph and relief, it now turned out that the new, modern arrangements, with their convenience and cleanliness, had another side — hard, frosty, pedantic, petty, and soul-destroying.

Before, when there had been a difficulty with something, you knew how much you would have to pay in bribes to overcome it. Now it was no longer a question of the price but of an endless toil of letters and papers, telephone calls and trips and talks, without ever knowing where they were leading and where they would end, for good or for bad.

And we were not young men, capable of adapting to any new thing. From day to day it became clearer to us how the old order had suited us and how the people who were no more had fitted our natures.

Perhaps I exaggerate.

At any rate, there was one among us who felt just like a fish in water: Luna's son was then in the prime of his youth. When he was absorbed in his studies, the books would leaf open before him of their own accord; and when he turned to his amusements, the street would spread out before him like a carpet; and when he jumped into the pool, the water would flee and he would pursue it.

He and Luna would come to the pool in the orchard, and during the hours I spent walking among the trees and arguing with the workers, while Daniel traipsed endlessly from one office to another in Tel Aviv and Jerusalem, these two would swim around each other in the water, diving and surfacing, splashing and spouting jets and again vanishing underwater, the goldfish in the pool fluttering around their legs, partly fleeing from them, partly seeking their company. If you like, it was an exhilarating sight; and, if you like, a terrible fear would grip me if I kept my eyes on what I saw for too long a time.

The son was about twenty-five during those days; but how old was Luna? The more I looked at her, the greater the doubt grew in me as to whether it was at all possible to know her age, and whether it was at all to be measured in years. Perhaps she was not born of woman at all, but of a process, one of the processes of time, without beginning and without end?

Had Daniel been with me here, in the orchard, during those days, when the son and his mother started coming here regularly, what would he have said?

I am quite certain that a father feels gratification when he sees his wife embracing and kissing her son; or when the son embraces his mother. But when did a father see what I saw in the orchard during those days? I will not say that I was alarmed at the very outset; the joy that two creatures take in each other has many aspects, and I had learned a lot from watching the bitch we had in the orchard playing with her pups, they climbing over her belly and wandering around among her teats.

As a person whose work is with the crops of the earth and the creatures of nature, I would not be surprised or amazed by numerous things most people would blush to see. And nevertheless!

Two or three years after the battles ended, when it seemed we had already attained tranquillity, the Arab refugees began shaking themselves out of their initial stunned amazement, and in the refugee camps in the neighboring countries, right on our borders, they started forming groups and infiltrating our areas to sabotage property, to steal, and to murder. And as much as we tried to place patrols and set up ambushes for them, we were unable to encompass the border of the entire State, and each night there were sounds of explosions, houses went up in the air, people were blown up and orchards set on fire. Then our people started devising strategies to frighten off the Arabs, and very soon the army started carrying out reprisal actions. If Arabs burst in from across the Jordanian border, our army would send a handful of men to the same place at night, to destroy and lay waste. And the same at the borders with Egypt, Syria, and Lebanon. Sure enough, Luna's son returned to the army and took part in those actions, and since he knew all the back roads in the land and the Arabic tongue flowed freely from his lips, he would penetrate deep into enemy territory without any fear. At times he would ride a horse three or four days' journey inside the Arab lands, and after some time he would return at night and cross the border back into our country, his face tanned and glowing.

Once, before he set out on such a trip, he came to take leave of his mother and kiss her, and as he held her face between the palms of his hands, he felt the earrings suspended from her earlobes.

They're ugly earrings, he said to his mother, smiling, and drew them carefully out of their places and threw them outside, through the window. I myself was present on that occasion and stared at him in surprise.

Not to worry, agronomist, he said to me. My mother has to be beautiful.

And thus he left us and did not come back for another three days.

When he came back, sweating and dusty, his face somewhat scratched, he entered the house at a time when we were seated for dinner. Before sitting down, he put his hand into his pocket and drew out a kind of bundle, something like a chunk of dried mud, and offered it to his mother. Luna took it into her hand, while we watched to see what he had given her.

She opened the bundle and dug into it with her fingers until its contents were visible. There were two big silver earrings there, of the kind worn by Arab women, the products of the jewellers of Hejaz or Sin'a.

And at the end of one of the earrings hung an earlobe, which had been torn from the body.

Daniel and I froze in our seats, but Luna kissed her son and got up and went into the bathroom, to return soon with the earrings — washed and polished — hanging from her ears, with a quiet smile on her face.

Now you're really beautiful, Mother, said the son.

18 Some of Daniel's Characteristics, Wherein Lie the Causes of Collapse

I am an old man today, alone and childless. The years left me in the land of the living are few and numbered. Not much time remains for me to understand what has been and to imagine what is yet to be after me. I strain with all my might to bring before my mind's eye all the things as they happened, but they insist on mixing together and erupting, refusing to lie still. Nevertheless I will not let them be. Perhaps I will yet manage to see straight. From the day my mind became deranged, in that cursed year of the locusts, there is no trusting me or my stories. But I will go on telling. Because if I don't tell this story, who will?

When I no longer had the slightest doubt about the mother and the son — and it was already clear that even if somebody were to put a stop to what was happening, nothing would help, because there are things that cannot be disregarded, even once they're stopped — even after all this, Daniel did not change his ways. Was he aware of what was going on around him? Or had these things never been, and was it only I who had woven or cooked up idle things in my feverish brain?

If that was so, why did Daniel stop coming to the orchard at night? Was it not because they — the mother and the son — had taken over the orchard for every night, every night of the year? Did I not see them coming towards evening, bathing in the pool, and then heading for the packing shed, gleaming in their nakedness in the darkness among the trees, and going into the room where Obadiah had coupled with her while he was still alive?

Had my mind gone completely? But I was both eye-witness and ear-witness. Those same sounds — which Daniel had heard or had imagined he heard when we sat together on the other side of the partition and eavesdropped — those same sounds I now heard myself with absolute clarity. And to do that I had no need to sit on the other side of the partition. From where I sat on the veranda I could hear them. And even when I went inside and closed myself in my room, the sounds came up through my windows.

At times I wanted to understand what they were saying to each other, but try as I might, I did not succeed. Even from a hand's-breadth away, when I pressed my ear to the wall, I could hear nothing but the sounds; in the end I imagined I heard voices singing, moving to a tune the like of which I had never heard in my life. Perhaps it was modern music, of the kind one sometimes hears on the radio, which the ordinary ear cannot enjoy. But it would be closer to the truth to say that it was an ancient melody, which had already passed from the world and been forgotten many centuries ago, to be resurrected now by these two. I am not well-versed in such things.

Now I would meet Daniel only during the daytime, when the work was plentiful and each of us was wholly immersed in it; yet I believe that it was not the orchard work that prevented us from speaking to each other, but the dread of the things we had to say to one another. Had Daniel asked for my advice then, it is possible that I would have said terrible things to him. Perhaps I would have told him to kill his son. I doubt whether I would have said this, though the thought would come back and offer itself to me night after night, and had I wanted to banish it from my mind, I would have had to beat my head against the wall and smash it.

Thus several more years passed.

And one spring morning in the year 1955, when Luna's son was almost thirty, it became clear to me that the end was drawing near. It was impossible for it to delay much longer, after what I had seen in Daniel.

He arrived at the orchard one day very early in the morning, and immediately upon getting out of his car he climbed the steps to my room and ordered me to close the door on the two of us.

The hole calls to the thief, he said, after sitting down in the armchair and fixing his agitated eyes on me.

I said nothing. I didn't know what he was talking about.

The orchard, Daniel went on from some hidden place in his mind, the orchard is too thick and too dark.

The orchard? I said. The orchard is too thick? But the densest part of our orchard has spaces of some five meters between trees. And we've even planted seven meters apart.

And nevertheless you can see, said Daniel.

What can I see?

You see that the orchard serves as a cover and a hiding place for all sorts of things that have no justice in them, said Daniel.

Justice? I repeated the word like an echo. I was alarmed and agitated.

Yes, no justice in them, he repeated his words firmly. I came to the land of my fathers so that I could live a life of justice and honesty, and look, what have I done? I have made a dark orchard, a sanctuary for wrongdoers. I murdered my brother in the orchard.

Daniel! I shouted. Daniel, this orchard yields fruit, and in each tree much toil and sweat and blood have been invested. Your blood, my blood. This orchard is all justice. All purity. All beauty, such as is not to be found on this earth. Daniel, what's wrong with you?

The orchard yields fruit, he said, but the fruit attracts the desires of the wicked; the orchard is too thick and too dark. We have worked too hard on it; it has become a hostelry for murderers.

And what do you propose? I said, a cold sweat covering my brow.

Perhaps we ought to thin it out a little, said Daniel softly, as if revealing a secret. Perhaps we ought to pull out a few trees, so they won't be ble to hide there, so that it'll be possible to see from one end to the other. So it'll be clearer. Things will clear up a little.

Thin it out? Pull up trees?

Perhaps burn it, Daniel whispered. If we burn it, bare trunks will remain, and it will be possible to see from one end to the other, and everything will be completely transparent and clear again.

I didn't have the strength to take what he was saying, and I burst out crying. Daniel looked at me, without even putting a hand on my shoulder to console me, smiled, and said: I see you've understood, and that you agree with me. Thank you, my friend, thank you, from the bottom of my heart.

I wiped my face with my hand and did not answer him. And so we sat there, silent until I suddenly noticed he was crying. I took a towel from the cabinet and moistened it under the tap in the kitchen, and then I stood over him, wiping his forehead and his face. Then I saw how his cheeks had become sunken and how many white hairs had appeared in his mustache of late, and I also saw that the light in his eyes was extinguished. It went out that morning, before my very eyes.

In our day people believe in doctors, thinking they can work miracles. It is not because the doctors are so wise that people believe in them, but because the understanding of people has become contracted, especially since despair has increased in their hearts. And after despair, only miracles can save. I don't believe in miracles; and if that day I called in a doctor for Daniel, I did so because I despaired of any salvation. Whatever had brought his illness upon him was fixed and anchored in infinite distances, where the hand of no man could reach.

Whoever pursues justice in the empty expanse of an orchard that is not his is bound to be exterminated. It is not the triumph of justice that will emerge as white as snow, but the bones of the pursuer that will be as wool, evaporating before the empty wind.

But he who masters life with joy, he will not sense or feel anything, even if the orchard is burned down around him. He will rejoice in the light of day just as he will sing in the darkness, because joy is his essence. And if I called the doctor, I did so in order to have no cause — then or ever — to accuse myself of daring to know what no man has the right to understand.

From that day on, I listened more intently than I had before, in the hope that I might hear what Luna and her son told each other when they coupled in the dead Obadiah's room. Had I been able to understand their talk, I would surely also have known the reason for Daniel's loss, and I would also have understood why fathers die and their sons inherit from them. At first glance this seems self-evident, but the truth is that nothing is self-evident. The fact is, we don't know a thing.

19 The End

What was not done to the orchard by the black rust or the red rust, the red spider or the Mediterranean fruit fly, the black knot or the Florida aphid, the mealy bug or the *Comestoc pseudococcus,* by bandits or enemies, by Turks, Arabs, or Englishmen, was done by Daniel, and more even. Daniel, who was blessed with wisdom, devotion, and love unparalleled in this world; Daniel, who had given his soul to the orchard day and night and had raised it to the highest imaginable level of agricultural achievement. Daniel, who brought to life, and Daniel, who brought to death. It was himself he brought to death. Just when the orchard reached the peak of its development, it became inhabited with ghosts for him. He began seeing the ghost of Obadiah wandering among the trees, and he would pursue this ghost, running over clumps and begging it for forgiveness, until he stumbled and fell, and the workers would carry him in their arms and deliver him to my room, just barely alive. And the things he would scream after this ghost — one could not hear them without horror. What guilt did Daniel not take upon himself? He said he had murdered him; he said he had stolen a wife from her husband's bosom; he said he was willing to give in, to retract, even to go back to the place he had come here from.

In those very days Luna became pregnant again. We all saw it, and Daniel saw it, too. I think Daniel believed that the child to be born would bring reconciliation with Obadiah's spirit, being a kind of memorial of the dead man, and that perhaps in the end he, Daniel, would be forgiven.

Thus — I think — Daniel mused to himself during those days; for otherwise, how can one explain what happened soon afterwards, when he went out among the trees and lay down in a ditch, where we found him the next morning, lifeless? By the lines of his face I could imagine that in his last moments he saw sights that put his mind at rest and appeased him. He would certainly have seen the trees shedding their leaves and the expanses spreading and clearing, leaving only naked trunks that no longer hid anything and only recalled the quarrel that had occurred here and that had now been settled so nicely — in final emptiness.

When the workers carried him and laid him down in the yard below the pool, I did not need to look toward the end of the row of trees opposite. Within myself I knew who was standing there, silently gazing at his corpse.

That morning we also learned Arab infiltrators had broken into the well-hut in our orchard and planted explosives, blowing up the pump we had once brought from Germany. This made Luna's son very angry, and he immediately linked thought to action. He took a rucksack with food, provisions for about a week, and a rifle with telescopic sights, and climbed to the top of a high water-tower looking out over one of the long roads leading east, and from his high position on the tower he took pot-shots at cars taking Arabs on their pilgrimages.

When the police brought him down, wounded by their bullets, his face was calm and serene, and it was then I saw how much he had come to resemble his mother in recent years.

He was sentenced to a year in prison, and in jail — where he was like a king in his castle, issuing orders and imposing his will on his jailers — he finished his studies, and soon after coming out received his degree as an aeronautical engineer.

And that same government of ours, which had sentenced him to imprisonment for going out to fight on his own initiative, learned a lesson from him. A year after his tower adventure, the government did what Luna's son had done, and went to war against the Egyptians, in 1956. It thus turns out that Luna's son anticipated his government by only one year.

The orchard lands were bought by speculators for good money, and soon surveyors will arrive there to subdivide them. Then the tractors will come to pull out the trees. After that they will dig foundations for houses, and some time later apartment houses will rise there, with electric posts jutting from their roofs and filthy garments waving in the wind from their balconies like the festival pennants of the city rabble whose clothes, even when they sleep, are loud in their garish colors.

New people will come gleefully to live in the new houses. And after a generation or two these people, too, will be dust and ashes. And the houses, too, will crumble. And in my mind's eye I see resurrection and destruction, destruction and resurrection, and it all has no end. Until the solver of riddles comes and solves this riddle, too, at the end of days.